AND NOBODY LIVED HAPPILY EVER AFTER

Kate Farrell

Parallel Universe Publications

First Published in the UK in 2015
Collection © Kate Farrell 2015
Cover © 2015

ISBN: 978-0-9932888-8-3
**Parallel Universe Publications, 130 Union Road,
Oswaldtwistle, Lancashire, BB5 3DR, UK**

Contents

INTRODUCTION

I first met Kate Farrell on Monday March 5th 1984 at a place called Petyt Hall, hard by Chelsea Old Church in London. I know this for a fact because I kept a diary, and for that matter still do. It was the first day of rehearsals for a major national tour of Garrick and Colman's play, *The Clandestine Marriage* in which we were both playing supporting roles to such theatrical luminaries as Joyce Redman, Roy Kinnear and Sir Anthony Quayle. Kate Farrell, or Kate David as she was then, was a bright young character actress with a gift for friendship and a sharp, humorous eye for the follies of her fellow actors. I, of course, had no idea then that I was encountering a future mistress of macabre fiction, the Countess of the *conte cruel*; but I thought I could detect in her a good sport, a "trouper" to use the old theatrical term, and I was right. Did she herself at the time have any intimations of her great literary destiny? I think not.

During the long tour of a play indelible friendships are forged, and sometimes indelible enmities. With Kate, happily, it was the former. 1984 was the year that Margaret Thatcher took on the miners and, as we made our way round England, the head of the company Anthony Quayle, expressed the pious hope that our tour to all four corners of the nation would help heal the great "North-South divide" that was being much talked about at the time. How Sir Anthony imagined that the performance of an 18th century comedy about aristocratic misalliances could oil the troubled waters of class hatred I do not know. Kate and I both thought that the idea was b – well, shall we say, a little far-fetched. We shared a distrust of that mixture of grandiosity, sharp practice and slightly glib bonhomie of which Sir Anthony was capable. A group of us, including Kate and myself, shared digs whenever we could. There were parties and laughter and gossip; we heard reports of Thatcher's war with Scargill and the miners, but it seemed a world away.

After the tour there was a West End run at the Albery Theatre and my friendship with Kate continued when that came to a close. Over the years we kept in touch. I began to devote more time and effort to writing. The theatre is a fickle mistress and life took both Kate and I in different directions. One day, perhaps, she will tell us of her experiences with the infamous Chuckle Brothers, but at some stage show business ceased to beckon for her as well. She too began to write and she sent me some of her stories.

I am generally wary of commenting on other people's unpublished manuscripts. What if they are no good? How does one gently tell a good friend that the writing of fiction is not for them? The stories Kate sent me were "His Family", "Mea Culpa" and an early version of "My Name is Mary Sutherland." I read them and I must admit my first reaction was one of immense relief: they were good, *really* good. No disingenuous words of faint praise were needed. I was impressed by the extraordinary assurance of the writing. Purple passages, wearisome clichés, vague and inconsequential digressions, indeed any sign of the amateur, all were entirely absent from her engrossing narratives. I should have known: Kate had always been the most professional of actresses; she was bound to be professional in whatever she took up.

But there was something much more important even than professional competence in her writing. She had a voice: crisp, shrewd, unsparingly honest, and rather elegant, despite the decidedly macabre subject matter. The people in her stories lived: they were vivid, recognisable; you might be unfortunate enough to meet them. You heard their voices and they seemed disturbingly familiar. The story telling was often uncommonly ingenious and surprising, as in "Mea Culpa," but the ingenuity was not just for show; it always had a purpose. I advised Kate to send some of her stories to Charlie Black, for inclusion in one of his splendid *Black Book of Horror* anthologies. He accepted them without hesitation, as I was sure he would, and the rest, as they say, is her story.

As you have probably just acquired this book what more need I say, really, except that you are in for an exceedingly entertaining and thought-provoking time from one of the most accomplished and original writers of macabre fiction alive today? If by any chance, you have not yet bought it, and are browsing through its pages, then what are you doing reading this introduction? You just have to go to the first paragraph of any of the stories here, and you will be hooked, but before you do, save yourself the discomfort of reading this book while standing up and probably pressed for time in a draughty bookshop. Buy the thing – it is exceptionally reasonably priced – put it in your pocket, go back home, make a cup of tea (or something stronger if you prefer) settle yourself in a favourite armchair and start reading.

You have done that? Congratulations! My job is done. But just in case you need a little further encouragement, let me say this. What distinguishes Kate Farrell's work is the extraordinary accuracy and vividness with which she sets up her situations. She has an eye for detail and an outstanding ear for the way people think and speak. It is far from fanciful to see this at least partly as the product of her experience as an actress. In the theatre, a natural faculty for observing one's fellow human beings is trained and honed. Listen to the narrator of "Waiting". If you don't know someone like that personally, you will have certainly heard her talking just behind you on a bus at some time. The intonation, the accent, the understanding, and the lack of it, are all so true to life. But the people Farrell evokes are not all from one social stratum, or one nation. Here is an ancient and corrupt Irish Priest ("The Way the Truth and the Life"), here is the wife of a notorious Argentinean dictator ("Las Cosas Que Hacemos por el Amor"), or the two Spanish schoolchildren in "The Efficient Use of Reason", and they are all done with the same conviction, the same ruthless accuracy. Farrell's eye is not heartless, but it is unclouded by any kind of sentimental affectation; her horrors emerge from what we sometimes call the commonplace. Very occasionally she touches on the supernatural, but when she does she does it superbly as in one of my favourites among her stories "A Murder of Crows" which shows that she can do an uncanny rural atmosphere with grim poetry as well as anyone. It is the gift of every worthwhile writer in this genre to make us realise that just beneath the surface of the banal and ordinary, there yawn great abysses of wonder and terror. I don't know quite why this realisation, in the hands of a writer like Farrell, should be so thrilling, enjoyable even, but it is. There is not a dull page, not a dull sentence in *And Nobody Lived Happily Ever After*.

And now, I suggest you waste no further time on studying this introduction, and embark at once on the seriously exciting business of reading Kate Farrell.

Reggie Oliver,
Suffolk, England, October 2015

MEA CULPA

Consider please, the theory of chaos: a butterfly flaps its wings in Japan, and here in London your lover tries to kill you.

Alex and I had been living together for four years. We were a handsome couple, both tall and fair, with strong profiles. Our high brows and patrician noses might have belonged on a coin and, like monarchs, we believed in never complain, never explain. We were occasionally taken for brother and sister, and as the idea of incest amused us, we would sometimes gently torture strangers with the notion that perhaps our relationship was not what it appeared. Our work was tolerable, our mortgage bearable, our friends genial, our families scattered. Child bearing and rearing was not yet an option, although we would consider the possibility and toy with names. I recall Clovis and Rapunzel were favourites for a while. It was more of a parlour game than a serious declaration of intent. Everything was perfection. Perfection: define it. A state of grace? Perhaps, yet that seems too Catholic. Is perfection the absence of badness or the presence of goodness? Goodness: again, define it. It would be possible, but not in the least desirable, to play these futile word games forever, or to become the armchair philosopher. The truth is that I find myself in a very strange place. I cannot recall how I arrived, and the ticket seems to have no return portion. That was careless of me.

For Alex and I, our home, our redoubt, was a split-level apartment in a converted warehouse, sublimely ill equipped to deal with children. As were we. There was a terrace, which overlooked a canal to the west of London, and in the cooler weather the smell from the water was barely perceptible. We loved the large windows, the oak floors, the soundproofed space where we could laugh, scream, twist and shout to our hearts' content, as the need arose. Most of all, we loved ourselves. Or so I thought.

Some months ago, Alex was holding the lift door open. It was an elderly if effective device with an interior concertina door, and as I entered, the door closed on my fingers. The pain, for a split second was like having teeth drilled without anaesthetic, my nerve endings were laid bare, and I thought I might faint. Alex looked at me, or through me, I couldn't decide which, as the pain had scrambled my vision. The next thing I recall was holding my hand under an ice cold running tap, with a suitably concerned Alex, ministering to my needs.

I heard, "Sorry, the door just slipped…" I was in no mood to care.

At work the next day, fingers swollen and taped up, I was reminded by the doom merchants that those old–fashioned lifts, though perfect in a Hitchcock film and wonderfully atmospheric, can be a death trap. I let some of the girls fuss over me, but didn't reveal how the door had actually slipped. I wonder why.

Alex cooked a superb meal by way of an apology, and it seemed better not to discuss the incident; incidents do happen, as surely as accidents. Who was it that said there are no accidents? Somebody. Besides neither of us cared much for soul searching, (never complain, never explain,) or angst ridden post mortems. And the food was to die for.

Several weeks later, as spring stuttered into summer, my fingers had healed and the incident was all but forgotten. I mentioned that a work colleague had invited me to play in a mixed doubles event at their tennis club. Alex hated tennis with a passion, so I had accepted the invitation without conferring. We would occasionally go our separate ways socially, as not all our interests were mutual. In fact that seemed to be one of the great strengths of our relationship.

"Sam Ryan's asked me to play in a mixed doubles thing on Saturday."

Alex followed a piece of Roquefort round the plate, pushed the plate away, eyed me.

"Ah, the lovely Sam. Am I invited too?"

"Christ no, you'd hate it, you hate tennis."

"I see." A sip from the wineglass. "So, you and Sam, and who else…?"

"Don't know. We've not played with each other before…"

"As it were," said my lover. I hated these cheap shots, so it was my turn to eye Alex; petty I know, but there is always room for small-mindedness, even in the grandest passion.

"Out with it," I said.

Alex stabbed at the cheese. What had it done to provoke such a mauling?

"I thought we were going to start work on the back bedroom?"

I held my ground, unaware of the shifting sands.

"We've been threatening to do that since Christmas, one more weekend won't make much difference. Anyway, I think I quite fancy the exercise."

The poor cheese was subjected to a further attack.

"Alright, you go and have your fun with Sam; you spend all week at work together, beats me why you'd want to spend the weekend too, but it's your choice." Cut, slash, stab. "I'll start the room on my own."

I loved Alex dearly, however interior decoration was not, what you might call, a strength. Plenty of enthusiasm, little finesse. I had designed our home with some care and flair with Alex as an occasional labourer, fetcher of brew and biscuits, and manipulator of stiff shoulders. Foolish, but I snorted with derision.

"Er, I don't think so…"

At that point, Alex plunged the cheese knife into the back of my hand.

Hindsight is not a benefit – it is a curse. Should I have been kinder, more appreciative, less impatient? Should I have been taller, shorter, older, younger, fatter, thinner? Can I recall a time I was aware of that subtle shift, which would later herald the tsunami? Was I that self-absorbed that Alex's needs were a poor second to mine? Was it all my fault? Yes, it must have been. I hadn't willingly or knowingly transgressed, I thought I had been charming, helpful, supportive, loving. I thought I had. With the benefit of this thing called hindsight would I have acted differently at any time? I don't think so.

There was no tennis that weekend.

That same Christmas, when we had discussed the redecoration of the spare bedroom, I had been the reluctant recipient of a Caithness paperweight, whose design resembled a lilac coloured foetus preserved in aspic. As it was a gift from Alex's purblind mother, it remained on display on a floating shelf, despite my periodic endeavours to consign it to a less prominent position. One Sunday, I was sitting reading the papers, or rather trying to. Alex had been overlooked for a promotion at work the previous week and as an unwitting by-product, eggshells had replaced the reclaimed floorboards in our apartment. I was aware of constant movement as I took cover behind the *Sunday Times*: pacing, swearing, endless cups of coffee.

Suddenly Alex said, "Catch!" and threw this paperweight at me. I was in mid fold of the property section, both hands were in play, and didn't manage to catch the projectile; instead I arrested its progress with my left ear. There was some swelling and considerable bruising, both of which ultimately healed. The headaches stopped eventually but a strange ringing continued in the ear, which my doctor thought may well be permanent.

After all these episodes there was remorse, a perfect meal or a carefully chosen gift by way of apology, and a promise of no repetition of the event. There were never tears, although there was gentleness. Doctors inspected injuries, we fabricated stories, and returned home to our halogen-lit battlefield. I loved Alex horribly. I wished to create no possibility of friction, I did the best I could to keep our relationship on an even keel, but each time I quizzed myself: what have I done to provoke these attacks? I remembered birthdays, and anniversaries; I enquired after Alex's harridan of a mother; I was punctual; I praised when necessary; I showed proper concern; I shared. It must have been something so subtle, some transgression that was imperceptible to any, other than Alex's keen eye. The fault must have been mine, and yet I was so afraid of further de-stabilising the fragility of the relationship that I did not dare ask. Life with these minor incidents was preferable to life without Alex.

Though the accidents were some months apart, friends and work colleagues were beginning to ask awkward questions, which I navigated as best I could. Strangely, I felt no need to unburden myself to anyone, and I found the only consolation I required was from Alex. As the summer sun poured into our home like molten butter and I closed the blinds on the giant windows, it was as if I was closing my eyes to the situation, and we settled to our life of disharmony without the disapproval or pity of outsiders. Last month, for instance, Alex and I were attempting to pass each other on the staircase when I carelessly lost my footing and slipped backwards down the last few stairs; it seemed simpler to take a few days off work, rather than explain my arm in a sling, and I was even able to make light of it, while being driven to hospital for what transpired was only a slight dislocation. And it served me right for wearing those ludicrous flip-flops.

"The nurses will be asking if I shouldn't get a season ticket," I said. Alex was not amused and no meal or gift, by way of apology was forthcoming. In fact, I apologised to Alex; it seemed a wiser course.

It could have continued; I refused to whine or indulge in bouts of self-pity, and I was ready to acknowledge that the fault was mine, and Alex's actions were as a result of my provocation. It could have continued, if I had not made the mistake of standing in the way when Alex was reversing the Audi. I was next to a pillar in the underground car park, thinking about theatre tickets I had reserved, *Othello* at the Globe, a perfect way to spend a summer's evening. It was a small apology for the incident on the stairs. Yes, I was aware of the car backing towards me, while Alex attempted a precarious manoeuvre in the confined space, and of course I did not assist matters by being so blatantly in the way, but nothing, nothing at all could have prepared me for the sensation as the bumper crushed my legs against the pillar, and then the boot pushed and crashed against my chest as I fell forwards. There was a moment of respite in that dimly lit car park, when Alex must have realised the mistake, and drove forward, releasing me. Was there a fault with the gears? The car reversed again, while I was still doubled over from the first impact. No, nothing could have prepared me for that. I was mashed – there is no other word for it – against the pillar again, my legs, my wrists, my forearms turned to liquid, and my ribs were reduced to splinters. My chest no longer seemed able to provide the wherewithal to breathe, which was baffling. One moment I was standing imagining Alex's delight when I produced the theatre tickets, and the next there was nothing but pain. The colour of pain is white.

Now I have plenty of time to contemplate the events that brought me to this place. What did I do wrong? It's a simple enough question, and until now one I was never brave enough to ask.

I lie here, stitched into my favourite Armani suit; it hides the devastation done to my body, which was broken beyond repair. The funeral directors reassembled the pile of sticks and mush that had been my torso; they padded and moulded to make me fit for viewing. Fortunately my face was unmarked, so Alex, my lovely Alexandra was able to bend over and kiss me goodbye. I felt her soft lips brush the light stubble on my cheeks, for it is true, the hair and beard do continue to grow after death. I know that now.

HELPING MUMMY

Martha was three. She had mink-soft brown hair, hazel eyes and the biggest smile. Her aim in life was to please, to please her parents, her grandparents and her small circle of friends. She was funny, helpful, interesting and interested, and everyone agreed she showed great promise in so many areas: her vocabulary was rich, her drawings worthy of any fridge door, and she could hold a pretty tune.

Unlike her brother Adam. He screamed some of the night and much of the day and aged thirteen weeks, already he was established as the family tyrant. When at his mother's breast, he was silent only long enough to suck and gnaw at the feeding station. God help the woman when teething began in earnest. He was not a pretty baby, with his ginger-blond fuzz and red face; the little thug's angry blue eyes blazed with the injustice of eviction from his nice, warm burrow once his thirty-nine weeks tenancy was up. His parents, David and Irene, were in a permanent state of readiness to soothe, to calm the infant, for despite the dimensions of their detached home the output from Adam's powerful lungs entered the neighbours' open windows like an unwelcome guest. Even nice Mrs Shapiro from two doors down admitted that she looked forward to the colder weather when the double-glazing would spare them the boychik's relentless repertoire. The boychik himself consumed his parents every waking hour and his father, a freelance journalist, enjoyed occasional nights out reviewing plays in town. The guilt he felt at leaving behind the pale, limp rag that his wife had become was assuaged by the first gin and tonic of the evening in some theatre bar.

Despite everything, David and Irene looked with

wonderment into their longed-for son's crib when he was settled, the day's battles forgotten. His bedroom became a demilitarised zone wherein hostilities were suspended, permitting his battle-scarred parents time to brace themselves for the next round of heavy artillery. Gazing upon him, they hoped he would reconcile himself soon to life in the outside world and prove a worthy playmate for their perfect daughter. There was little to compare with the stillness of their sleeping infant: the small chest rising and falling, tiny fists curled, at peace. Irene would lean over to check Adam was still alive, so soft was his breathing. The tranquillity was tangible. She wished that she could snap off a piece and have it for a treasured keepsake. In such benign moments she and David wondered if Adam would have her father's looks, or his father's healing hands. My son the doctor, she mused.

On any evening while the scene of parental devotion unfolded upstairs, downstairs Martha, ready in her nightdress, would contemplate her latest artwork. This might well be a picture of the baby dressed as a pirate or a king. Certainly it was another masterpiece to add to the collection on the front of the fridge freezer. At this rate soon her works would be adorning the washer dryer too.

Before her brother's arrival on the scene, these precious minutes were shared with her mother and sometimes her father. Her pre-Adam period featured the three of them posed outside a red or yellow house on a green sward with a slash of blue sky at the top. The jolly trio stood, stick fingers touching as if holding hands, with her small self always in the middle. She added a dog, but Irene and David never took the implicit hint, and came home one day with a baby brother instead. She never included Adam in any drawings with his family, though he featured in a fine collection of portraits in his own right. What would a child psychologist have made of it?

One day in the autumn, when Irene was too fraught to

notice the turning of the leaves, David packed an overnight bag and took a cab to King's Cross. With some reluctance he was travelling to York to review a play and would be staying away one night only. Irene insisted she'd be fine with the kids. It's old York, not New York, so go, she said, and at least you'll get an unbroken night's sleep. They suffered as one. Martha did a special drawing of Daddy on a train for him to take along for company. She was thoughtful, considerate beyond her tender years, and worried that he might be lonely without them.

When the taxi arrived at half past eight in the morning David's small family stood watching from the doorway. Martha waved like a cheerleader while a yawning Irene held in her arms the struggling savage that was their son.

Their day continued as usual. The cleaning lady came, polished, vacuumed, and went, and Irene did the three daily loads in the washer dryer; Adam surveyed and ranted from his baby bouncer; Martha pretended to press her dolly's clothes on her toy ironing board, a gift from her grandmother that Irene felt was an uninspired choice, though she no longer had the energy to complain about such things.

"See, Mummy, I'm helping, aren't I?"

"Yes, darling, that's nice."

"I'm ironing Daisy's dresses, aren't I, Mummy?"

Martha had developed the tendency of turning everything into a question, a habit that had evolved only since Adam's arrival. Her parents hoped she would soon tire of it, though she showed no signs yet. And it was only *slightly* annoying.

"Look, Daisy" – this was directed at her favourite doll, – "I'm doing the ironing to help Mummy, see?"

After lunch when the final load had been removed from the dryer, Irene curled up on a large leather sofa. She would change Adam's outfit presently. The little emperor could just wait for once. Ignoring only the slightest frisson of guilt, she riffled through the pages of the celebrity gossip magazine that the cleaner had left. Irene hadn't opened a decent work of fiction in over three months. The Beckhams, the Hurley-Warnes, the Pitt-Jolies, the babes, the dudes, all melded into one many-headed hydra and she thought, "If I just close my eyes for a minute..."

Her children were out of harm's way. Adam wobbled in his bouncy chair, bashing at the toys suspended in his eye line. At thirteen weeks he hated clowns already. He had lunched on the finest his mother's breast could provide, and was not at that moment crying or complaining. Martha played at her toy stove, and Irene could watch them both from the comfort of her sofa. That is she could have watched them, had her eyes been open and had she not succumbed to the deepest of post-lunchtime slumbers.

Martha rattled the plastic eggs round on the mite-sized frying pan. When they were ready she slid them onto a plate, just like Mummy, and carried them carefully over to the sofa.

"Mummy, look, I've made you something nice to eat, haven't I?"

Irene's head had dropped to the side, her mouth was slightly open and a triple snore like three little piggies escaped. Oink, oink, oink.

"Mummy?"

Her mother muttered in her sleep and settled further down in the sofa, while the Beckhams and the rest slid to the floor. Martha picked up the magazine and left it on the coffee table for amongst her many virtues she was also tidy. Mummy obviously wasn't going to play kitchens, so Martha, though disappointed, retired to her corner and settled to some crayoning.

Adam chose that moment to revert to type. The lower lip was thrust forward, the features puckered, and the mouth opened for one of his operatic bellows. Martha waggled a finger at him, just like when she had cause to remonstrate with dolly.

"Shhhh, Adam, Mummy's asleep."

Adam didn't care, he wasn't a considerate baby. Although the second child, he was the first son of David and Irene Saltman, and he knew his rights. His unassailable role as the Saltman heir was hardwired into his DNA. He swatted at the felt clowns that so enraged him, and bawled anew. Martha stood over him in his bouncy chair and tried to reason with him.

"Shhh now, be a good boy. Mummy's sleeping."

By way of response he took a deep breath and marshalled his resources for another scream.

Martha did what she had seen her mother do: she felt Adam's bottom through his nappy. He was wet.

Baby's wet, Mummy's asleep. Something had to be done.

Martha wriggled the infant out of his seat and half carried, half dragged him the short distance into the utility room. She concentrated hard.

Luckily, Mummy had left the door to the washer dryer open when she had removed the final load. Martha had to huff and puff a bit to get her brother up over the rim, but once he was inside the washer she was able to shut the door which had a soft closing mechanism so no sound escaped to waken Mummy. Unsure which buttons to press she placed a small hand over the control panel and activated several at once. The machine murmured into life and Martha stood back, relieved that her exertions had not been in vain. She took a final look at Adam behind the glass as the water level started to rise. His small red face was contorted with rage or perhaps some other emotion. As there was no sound, it was difficult for her to judge. Satisfied, she returned to her crayons. Mummy would be so pleased when she saw how Martha had helped!

Some time later Irene awoke. She lay for a moment listening to the unwonted silence of the house. However as she came to full consciousness she was aware the silence wasn't absolute. There was the distant mumble of something mechanical. Had she left a radio on somewhere? Was it the dishwasher from lunch? Perhaps the washer dryer in the utility room? She stirred herself as it was time to check on the children; hopefully she'd find her daughter drawing in some quiet corner, and the boy sleeping in his bouncy chair. He occasionally did if she was being particularly blessed, and this must be one of those rare times. The poor little mite would be soaking and would need changing, of that she was certain.

Irene went into the kitchen. Yes, there was Martha, her small head bent over another masterpiece.

"Mummy fell asleep, naughty Mummy! What's my girl been up to then?"

"Helping Mummy," said her first born. "And drawing. See, Mummy? It's Adam."

Irene inspected Martha's handiwork. It looked like a square with buttons at the top, and there was a wonky circle in the middle with possibly a face drawn on it. Then she looked at the empty bouncy chair, wherein she had placed her son.

She heard the whoor-whoosh-slish-slosh from the utility room. There was a crump-thump too. When David put his running shoes in the washer, it made that very sound as the unaccustomed weight was raised and dropped back.

"Adam? Where's Adam?" she asked somebody. Anybody.

"Adam," she said once more, as if by merely saying the name he would magically appear in his little chair.

A finger of iced water began its desolate journey down Irene's spine.

The rhythm of the whoor-whoosh-slish-slosh-crump-thump drew her towards the utility area and she looked down into the washer dryer.

There was some misshapen and swollen thing spinning and turning in the machine's drum. She had found her son.

She made out small hands slapping against the inside of the glass door, and something that might have been Adam's head. Might have been. Hard to tell.

Martha joined her mother, placing her hand in Irene's. She smiled up at her.

"I've been helping, haven't I, Mummy?"

"Mummy?"

It was autumn and the windows were closed but even nice Mrs Shapiro from two doors down was able to hear Irene.

A MURDER OF CROWS

They used to say that if you listen very hard you can hear a slight scratching in the earth. Scratching is perhaps not the word; it's a murmur, and a twitch, then a small rustle. It only happens after the barley has been harvested in Mitchell's field during a six-week spell from mid September until late October. Listen as if your life depended on it, they would say. As well it might. Only the particularly gifted can hear it even though we all have the chance, and if you don't try you won't know. Most go to their graves without ever knowing. But not all.

When I had long chestnut hair and a smile I was told that would brighten the darkest room, I heard this murmur twitch rustle. I had been away from the village for years and had returned, a woman ripe with ideas and education, to care for my ailing mother. Such was my lot as an only child. The career as an advocate, the fine apartment in the city and the man, they waited for me. In my charmed life many things were possible.

The first time of Hearing I thought it was the wind because here on the East coast we are prone to fierce gusts as the weather draws up her skirts before the winter. I discounted it. And the second time I thought it was because the music from a ceilidh was still sounding in my ears. And the third time I hardly paused for I was hurrying to see my childhood friend Morven. Or to be precise her baby, the bonny handsome boy who so liked to curl his fat finger about mine. I loved to stroke his cheeks and his ludicrously tiny nose; one day soon I would be bringing a little playmate to visit him, my own child. But it was early yet and so he or she was still my secret. Not even the father knew.

The fourth time however I stopped and listened. I leaned

over the wall and looked deep into Mitchell's field, as if looking hard would heighten my powers of hearing. It seemed more insistent than the previous times when I had barely acknowledged it. Maybe it wanted me to hear it. Some tale from my childhood, like a rat in a trap, gnawed and worried at the back of my mind. Was it daring me to remember? Was it trying to tell me something? I listened. There was not a breath of wind. Stripes of cloud like soiled rags hung across the moon, unable to stay or go. I looked deeper into the field at the ruts and trenches of the flattened barley stumps, painted mouse brown in the moonlight. Murmur twitch rustle. The Stirring.

Back at my mother's house, I assisted her to bed. What had delayed me, she wanted to know, though not unkindly. My mother had not an unkind thought in her head, nor a mean bone in her body, a body that was diminishing with every week as the disease devoured her.

Sorry, mam, I said. Here I always called her 'mam', though when I spoke of her to city friends she became 'mother.' I was passing Mitchell's field, and heard the strangest noise, I told her. I'd heard it before and hadn't paid much attention, but for once I stopped and really listened. It was like I forgot time, I said. Being back in the village did that to me, it sucked out the city life attitudes from my brain.

Mam's hand rested on my arm; she seemed to be pinning me into place with a strength I wouldn't have thought possible. Her other hand fretted at the blanket, pecking at the edges.

This noise? Can you describe it?

No, I said, not really, it's hard to put into words.

And you with the education, said my mam.

Yes, me with the education.

Was it a scratching sound, she asked?

Scratching? Well, yes, it could have been. A scraping maybe, or rustling.

She sighed as if her over-educated, highly qualified daughter was just some silly, addle-headed goose of a girl.

You really don't remember, do you? The tale about the crows? The Hearing?

Her words opened a door in my memory. Tired though she was, she told once again the story all we children learned as soon as we reached the age of understanding:

The Mitchell family had owned the farmland at the edge of the village for generations. A long narrow stripe of it separated two halves of the village and for ten months of the year all were free to come and go taking the narrow path that provided a short cut. No damage was done, it was only the local residents as few strangers visited, and the Mitchells permitted the access. The soil was quick and fertile, perfect for continuous barley growing, however once the harvest was in there was no crossing it, no detours were possible for almost two months of the autumn. For it was said that was when the young crows had their Birthing. In the autumn, mind, not the spring. And not nesting in the trees, for they were being hatched from under the earth! And always at night-time. The following days the ground was often flecked with feathers shed during this rogue nativity.

Many years before, a young woman called Lorna Blair was blessed with the Hearing. She was married to Tom Mitchell, a loveless but pragmatic union arranged by her father and Thomas Mitchell the Elder, over a handshake and a glass or two. It was for the mutual benefit of both families. Young Tom was strong as a bullock and slow-witted, Lorna was bright, passionate and pretty. Her heart belonged to another and so did her body. While heavy with her lover's child, she ignored the warning, and disregarded the Hearing and the Stirring; some said she was running away with him. Whatever her reasons she tried to cross the field and was frightened into premature childbirth by a flock of birds who descended around her. These were the adult crows come to protect the birthing place of their young. Jabbing and scything at her, she was hidden by the black oily cloud of their wings. The lucky ones, they feasted on her eyes, as if prizing the gelatinous orbs. Her blood flowed onto the ground, and the crows bathed in it, fed on it. She died, and also the torn and shredded infant within her.

And so it was the field gave birth to more crows, the chicks came from under the earth, not from nests and not bursting from eggshells. It began with a soft crackling sound, then feathers as dark as an inky moonless sea would gradually appear. First a few, then many, as they thrust their way upwards into the air.

The cycle continued. In family after family, the story was told to all the children of the village. Not all were blessed with the Hearing, but if you were you had to resist crossing the field, until All Hallows Eve. If you were blessed, for few were, then anything might be in your grasp. All believed, even the incomers learned to recognise the truth of it. Whether it was 'the divil's wark' no-one would say.

Exhausted then from recounting this ancient tale with its dire warnings, the light dimmed in Mam's pale grey eyes so I settled her down, our bedtime roles now reversed because of her age and her illness. I smiled at the story and its memory however. What a piece of superstition and foolishness it was, yet guaranteed to give the village children nightmares. I would tell my friends when I was back in the city, and would raise a laugh with the nonsense in some chic wine bar. They said I was a country girl at heart. They said I could be fey at times.

Not so long after this, I was out another evening and I remembered to my shame that it was my man's birthday and I hadn't even sent him a card. I had checked the stock at the village store and found them not even bad enough to send as a joke, and somehow I never made the journey to find something suitable elsewhere. You see I lost the time too easily when back home. I decided I would call from Mam's, sing Happy Birthday, and promise him a fine time when I was with him once again. Soon, it would be soon. I loved my mother sure, but this was not the life I'd planned for. Not this. Not here.

It was nearing midnight, soon his special day would be over and I needed to get back fast, so using the moon as my lantern, headed for Mitchell's field to shorten the passage. As I began the journey across it that night in late October, I was thinking only of my man, and how for his next birthday there would be a son or daughter to add to his happiness. Maybe I ignored the murmur twitch rustle, or maybe I didn't hear it. It is hard to recall.

Yet what I can recall is the swoop, the sudden rush, the thrashing of wings, the violin shriek of the crows as they shrouded me in the mass of their black cloak; I recall how my clothes screamed as the fabric was torn; I recall the silver ice-pick of the pain, the burned copper tang of the blood, and my mouth filling with worms from the mud; I recall the stabbing into my skull, while the birds' claws grasped at gore streaked clusters of my hair; I recall my hands reduced to shreds as I tried to fend them off. And I recall the fury of their beaks raking at my body, my belly, my baby. There was no crying out, my tattered throat was incapable of sound. After the initial frenzy an unholy calm descended and in the comparative silence I heard them eating me. And yes, the lucky ones feasted on my eyeballs.

Now many years later, I sit here in my mother's house, though now of course it is mine. They found me in the field. Like Lorna, my blood had flowed into the earth. Those who crossed the ground to help me in the morning they were safe, for it was All Hallows Eve. I was taken to the city. I was patched and stitched and after some months had passed, I was nearly repaired.

The career, the apartment and the man were no longer possible. He was kind for a short while. Strangely though, I remember him saying that I wasn't to worry about the loss of the baby as he wasn't ready for fatherhood just yet, and besides it was something we hadn't even discussed. And I thought I knew him. Barely a year after, I learned he found himself a woman who was whole and they named their son Matthew. I returned to my mother's home, too late for her obsequies. Was it the shock of me that killed her, I asked, and not the disease? Nobody answered.

They say I was lucky to be saved. I have somehow put a life back together, though the village children run from me, or so I am told. I can neither see them nor speak to them, yet I hear them as I tap around the village. Oh yes, I hear them. I listen for the murmur twitch rustle though I have not heard it again, so I hold onto the vain hope that if it should present itself I might somehow force myself onto the cursed stripe of land for the birds to finish me off.

I wait.

I wait until it is my time when I will join my mother, my baby, the others.

NO JUNK MAIL

Judith Webster lived alone in a nineteen-thirties built, semi-detached house, number 63, Arragon Gardens, Streatham. She had done for seven years since her husband Geoffrey died. She didn't mind her solitary status for her life was full: she went to painting classes, studied cake decoration at evening school, joined the bridge club, sang in a local choral group and did voluntary driving for Trinity Hospice, as the staff there had made her husband's final weeks tolerable, for both of them. A pleasant life. Especially without Geoffrey.

But.

There is often a 'but'.

Like many of us she had her pet hates. These included children who rode their scooters in shops, any form of cheese, and the use of the rising inflection at the end of a sentence. "Are you asking me or telling me?" she would enquire. At the very top of her list however was the receipt of junk mail, in fact unsolicited matter of any sort. It was a broad church and included the small cards for mini cab firms, and flyers from the Light of Bengal/Pearl of the Orient/Vesuvio's Speedi Pizzas; gardening services and anything else that smacked of home improvements; electioneering pamphlets and collection bags for charities; property papers, the local free gazette, and even the monthly newsletter from the Methodist chapel. All of them incurred her ire.

On a postcard she wrote in upper case: **NO JUNK MAIL**, in bright crimson letters on white card and underlined it for good measure. She had been to WH Smith to purchase coloured pens especially and opted for red. She liked the implications: red for danger, red rag to a bull, seeing red, and wedged it behind the clear glass panel in her front door. It was hard to miss. A friend suggested she should use the old favourite: "No Hawkers, Canvassers, or Circulars" and offered to print something from her computer, laminate it, make it look smart, business-like even, but Mrs Webster preferred the hand made, slightly amateurish approach. Her lettering started out big and bold but the final 'i' and 'l' were compacted to fit on the card.

"No, it's short and to the point. No junk mail. That's simple enough. Besides I don't want it to look too neat; for all these buggers know, a right lunatic might live here, someone mad enough to handwrite a sign and not care what it looks like." And she added: "Not all of them speak English you know," as if it were a crime.

For a while it worked. That is to say there was a slight decrease in unwanted ephemera. But there would still be times when she'd come back from a bridge date with the girls, or a shopping trip to the Whitgift Centre in Croydon, and find a slip of paper from the Punjabi Palace, offering free delivery and free nan bread if you spend over £30; or perhaps it would be The Computa Doc.ta (sic), who could sort out an ailing PC in the comfort of your own home. Or the glossy property magazine from an estate agent.

"Bloody hell. Can't these morons read?" she would ask the universe.

If she happened to be downstairs and the letterbox rattled long after the postman's visit, she would march quick smart to the front door. Removing the offending article from her mat, she would then fling open the door and harangue whoever was slow in his or her retreat down the garden path. One unfortunate pamphleteer from the Lib-Dems was tackled thus:

"Can you read English?"

"Yes, of course."

"What does it say?" She directed his attention to her handwritten sign.

"This isn't junk mail," he said, "it's electioneering for

30

the council elections."

"It is unsolicited, therefore it is junk."

"Don't you want to know what's happening in your community?"

"Excuse me?"

"Don't you want to know what's going on out there?"

"I'm more than aware what is going on out there, thank you very much, and you'd do well not to try and patronise me on that score. I was voting long before you even dreamed about taking a degree in political sciences or meed-ja studies, or whatever they call it now. So please take this piece of rubbish away, or I shall have to tell your candidate that one of his canvassers needs to work on a) his manners and b) his comprehension skills, and explain therefore why he won't be getting my vote."

At which point said canvasser withdrew.

Other exchanges were less protracted and the opening salvo was usually, "Can you read?" Or perhaps, "You've dropped something," though she felt that was just a bit too subtle. Her current favourite was: "What part of No Junk Mail don't you understand?"

She was sometimes greeted with a shrug, a slight apology, or just an outstretched hand to take back the offending item. However after many, many weeks, she was amazed that leaflet droppers *still* came to her door and ignored the sign. But came they did.

During a long, fine spell of weather she worked in her back garden, even though bending over sometimes left her breathless, as she was neither young nor slender. It had been Geoffrey's domain and, driven by pragmatism, she took over its maintenance rather than live in a suburban wilderness and rather than pay someone. "Why keep a dog and bark?" she asked her bridge partner. She left the front door open while she toiled and weeded and deadheaded and tidied, and was therefore in pole position to tackle any unsuspecting leafleteer, irrespective of age, race, colour, creed or political persuasion. Anyone who was reckless enough to drop his or her publicity material on her mat was fair game.

Twelve-year-old Dev Sharma, small for his age, was in her sights on more than one occasion. As he left a most colourful handout for his uncle's car hire company, one of her comments to him was:

"For Christ's sake, don't they teach you people to read at school nowadays? What am I paying taxes for?"

His older sister operating on the opposite side of the road led her confused sibling away and reported the incident to their uncle when back at base.

This particular fine and sunny day, one of her nastier outbursts was directed at Iracema, a young woman from Belo Horizonte. Her HomeHelp flyer offered assistance with house cleaning/babysitting/dog walking. She had leaned in and dropped it on the mat, as the door was open at 63 Arragon Gardens.

As she trudged down the path back towards the garden gate, this homesick Brazilian heard:

"Oi, you."

She stopped and turned to see, appearing from round the side of the house, a red-faced woman perhaps in her mid sixties; her hair was scraped into an unbecoming ponytail and there were smears of soil across her furrowed brow and her florid cheeks. Two passing schoolboys sniggered.

"Where's yer wigwam, Geronimo?" the bolder one hooted.

"I know where you go to school, you little snots. Now bugger off."

"Ooo-ooo-oooh!" was the rejoinder, but they moved off quickly nonetheless.

Mrs Webster turned her attention back to her primary target.

"You there. Can you read? Can you read English, to be

exact?"

Before Iracema could reply the woman continued:

"No. Junk. Mail. Look," and pointed at the sign on the open door.

"No junk mail," Iracema read.

"Ah, so you can read English then?"

"I didn't see it." Which she hadn't.

"Bit hard to miss, don't you think?"

Iracema took the piece of paper back from the woman. It was now crumpled, too tatty to put into anyone else's door. She moved away down the path saying quietly, "Sorry, it won't happen again."

Mrs Webster missed the crucial first word, the slight apology; her ears only caught a muttered comment.

"Excuse me?" she barked. "What did you just say?"

"It won't happen again."

"Too bloody right it won't," said the red-faced woman. "And shut the gate. We get all sorts around here. Bloody gyppos."

Iracema had not had a good day. Her landlord told her he would have to raise her rent by ten pounds a week, and the photocopying machine she used at a corner shop developed a fault and had gobbled up several of her precious flyers. Worst of all, an interview loomed for she had been summoned to appear before the Border Agency as she had been in the country for eight months. And now the red-faced woman. She didn't need it. Not any of it.

"Eu odeio este país," she told the pavement, that was pocked with hardened chewing gum. Nobody cared. What was the point? She was alone.

The world of the leaflet dropper was a strange and a solitary one. They rarely operated in pairs, it was just a man or a woman with a rucksack or a satchel containing their message: Eat me. Try me. Call me. Hire me. Many of them had MP3 players for company, plus a bottle of water or a thermos. Chocolate, unless it was too hot, dried fruits, yoghurt covered raisins, any form of portable sustenance that didn't take up too much space in the backpack. They would skate, glide, pedal, stroll or march around the neighbourhoods, ignoring blocks of flats (broken lifts and too much abuse for too little return,) and target suburban houses, leaving their paper trails. Sometimes they crossed each other's paths, sometimes not; sometimes they smiled, acknowledging the others, sometimes not. Iracema of 'HomeHelp', Graham of 'Gutted, THE Gutter Cleaners', Mr Sharma of 'Excelsior Cars', Kelvin of 'Vesuvio's Pizzas' and Jarek of 'Rainbow Painters and Decorators,' would greet each other on occasion. A nod. A genial grunt. A small wave. They might even stop and exchange pleasantries on Streatham Common, content to pause in the middle of their leaflet drops and pass a few moments in each other's company. They would briefly compare backgrounds and dreams and aspirations, often in fractured English. Names were seldom exchanged, thus Mr Sharma was 'Excelsior,' Kelvin was 'Vesuvio,' and so on.

On this day, Mrs Webster's volley of abuse proved to be Iracema's undoing. She slumped onto a garden wall, well away from number sixty-three, and sighed. The sigh travelled from the soles of her feet via her weary soul and was dispelled in one long breath as she sat, shoulders sagging. On the other side of the road, Mr Sharma appeared at that moment, and waved as he saw her. He was about to call out but took immediate stock of the situation, and read the body language of one very unhappy young woman.

He crossed to her side and leaned over, shading her from the sun, and studying her slightly greasy hair as it fell over her face. She was thin and pale, not at all his cup of tea, but she was a fellow traveller on life's journey and merited some show of concern.

"Hello, HomeHelp. Are you ill?" he asked.

She looked up; he looked down, and saw tears

cascading down her cheeks.

"Oh dear, oh my goodness, what is wrong? Here. Have some tea." He always carried round a thermos in his leaflet satchel; Assam, fine, strong tea.

He poured her some and handed her the inner cup from the thermos lid; he always had the two cups in case he ran into anyone he knew.

She sipped, then sighed. Then cried, then sipped some more. He sat on the wall beside her and waited for information. As he waited, a third member of their little band cycled down the pavement into view. This was Jarek the decorator. He had come from round the corner and also suffered a tongue lashing from Mrs Webster.

"Friends! Hello. Are you having party?" he asked, as they drank their tea. He was always up for a good time.

"HomeHelp is upset," said Mr Sharma, stating the obvious. "But we don't know why," he added.

"So, no party," said Jarek, scratching his chin. He joined them on the wall. "You tell me perhaps?" he said to Iracema. Mr Sharma was nonplussed, for he had arrived first and had offered her his tea.

"Yes, miss, you tell us," he said.

Iracema wiped her nose on the back of her hand and left a snail trail on it.

"It's nothing. No. It's everything. I hate it here. I want to go home but I can't. I try to save for airfare. I hate my landlord, I hate my room, and I hate that woman round the corner."

"Ah" said Mr Sharma.

"Oh," said Jarek.

They knew who she meant.

"Number sixty-three?" asked Mr Sharma.

"Blue door with sign on it?" asked Jarek.

"Red-faced woman say do I speak English? She was very rude. She screw up my paper. I speak English good. I read Harry Potter." Iracema had recovered sufficiently to register her indignation.

"I come from there just now," said Jarek. "The door was open and I left a card on the mat but she came out as I did it, and say to me, 'Not another of you lot. Can't any of you read,' except she say the effing word too. Mouth like a sailor, I think. I say to her, this is not junk mail, not if she needs a man to paint her house, this is important."

Here Mr Sharma nodded in agreement. His mini cab company might prove to be her salvation one day if there was a train strike and she needed to be at Gatwick Airport. No, it's not junk mail. They are offering a service, and a crucial one at that. He explained this to the others and they were all as one on that particular issue.

"Anyway," finished Jarek, "she tell me to go away, she'll be the judge of what's important. Except she did not say 'go away', she tell me to fuck off. Sorry, friends. And when I go away on bike, she say and get off the fucking pavement, pavement for walking. She is old lady, it's not nice."

They all paused to think of other old ladies, their respective grandmothers: Iracema's in Belo Horizonte, Jarek's in Gdansk and Mr Sharma's in Leicester.

"I know this woman too, she frightened my nephew," he said. "He won't do the leaflets any more. I said well, don't go to her house, but he thinks she might catch him in the road, might tell her friends. He's a good boy, small for his age, and he's well, he's not quite all there, you might say. Special needs, they call it. My brother is worried sick about him, I may as well tell you. We all are. This woman at number sixty-three, she set him back."

Jarek and Iracema absorbed most of this information, and nodded.

"She is a monster," declared Iracema.

"She is bad person," concurred Jarek.

"Something should be done," stated Mr Sharma. His companions nodded. "She has no respect for human dignity, no consideration. She should eat her words."

At which point, Mr Sharma's face was suffused with a strange and wonderful light, even on that bright afternoon. A ready solution!

He rose from the wall, put the cups back on his thermos and straightened his satchel over his shoulder.

"No, instead she should eat *our* words," he said. "Come." His companions looked at him, at each other and shrugged. What did he mean?

She should eat *our* words?

Mr Sharma took one of his mini cab cards, opened his mouth as if to make a meal of it, then mimed eating.

"Yes?" was all he said.

Iracema and Jarek were educated people, they understood at once what Mr Sharma meant, and so armed and dangerous with sheaves of leaflets and flyers, they went back round the corner to number sixty-three. As they approached the house, it began to cloud over; the best of the day was behind them. Sunshine was now replaced by greying skies, and a distant rumble of thunder meant the day's leafleting was drawing to its natural conclusion.

Mrs Webster had finished her gardening and retired indoors for coffee and chocolate digestives. She was expecting a delivery of a new blade for her mower and sat in her kitchen listening out for a knock at the door.

When it came, and when she went to answer it, she was surprised to see, not the livery of the man from Parcelforce, but a motley trio, two men and a girl. The girl and one of the men, a tall white man wearing jeans and a tee shirt, she recognised. The second man was shorter, Indian, Arab, or something, who also looked familiar though she was not sure why. From the newspaper shop, most likely. The couple though, oh yes, she had seen them both off her property not an hour since. What part of the exchanges with her had they not understood? She had been graphic enough, she thought. She suspected all along they were morons.

"Christ Almighty, what the hell do you lot want?" she growled.

The Indian stood in the middle and appeared to be their spokesperson.

"Lady, please..." was all he said, before he pushed her back into her hallway ever so, ever so gently. Just like the playground bully when challenged, surprise overcame her, and she stumbled backwards as the second man closed the door on them. She stood in her hallway with three total strangers; harmless looking individuals but their method of entry had shocked her. All this took mere seconds from opening her door, to the flash of recognition, to the brief exchange between herself and the Indian, or whatever he was. Other than outrage she had little time to register anything for the three bore down on her waving various pieces of paper. Small mini cab cards, photocopied leaflets for a domestic service of some sort, and other flyers with a clipart logo of a rainbow and a paintbrush.

Mrs Webster opened her mouth to order them off her premises but got no further than the intake of breath. Led by the little Indian (or was he Arab?) her opened mouth was stuffed slowly and methodically by each of the three with their paperwork.

"Whaaaaagghh...?" she managed, between shreds of paper.

"No, lady, you eat *our* words now. You have upset my friends here, and my family, you are a rude person, ungenerous."

"You are monster, bad, bad woman," added Iracema, as she crumpled up another of her handbills to force feed the woman at number sixty-three.

"You have dirty mouth," Jarek told her, placing some balls of rainbow coloured paper in her mouth that was now wedged open. It was only at this point that Judith Webster's common sense kicked in as the initial shock of

38

this outrage diminished, and she leaned over and started to try and spit out the mush onto the hall floor, reaching in her mouth to remove wads of paper.

Mr Sharma, indicating the small piles of sputum softened material, remarked to Iracema, "Now the lady will need cleaning service for sure!"

In what had thus far been a truly miserable day, this was the first ray of sunshine for the Brazilian girl, and she began to laugh and laugh and laugh. She threw back her head, showing her small misshapen teeth and laughed and hooted and howled. Jarek had a good soul. When people cried, he cried and when they laughed he joined in, without always knowing the cause. So he too guffawed and bellowed and the noise ricocheted round Mrs Webster's hallway, a demented symphony of merriment, while the woman was bent double and continued to spit.

Mr Sharma smiled, watched as Jarek pulled the woman up and held her arms behind her thereby allowing Iracema and himself access to their victim's mouth once more.

"Yes, lady you keep on eating our words. Yum yum yum," Mr Sharma said as he and the girl continued their feeding.

The more Mrs Webster tried to spit out the paper mush, the faster the benign little Indian gentleman and the Brazilian girl fed her. The pieces of mini cab cards began to cut at the insides of her mouth and she tasted blood. It was not possible to hawk out the lumps, as they were squashed into her face as soon as she managed to dislodge a small amount, and with the tall man holding her hands there was no possibility of pulling out the plugs. She tried to swallow some bits at which Mr Sharma pronounced his delight to his companions as her gullet rose and fell.

"Look, friends, it works! She is eating finally."

Swallowing didn't help at all, so Mrs Webster, strong and supple enough for a woman in her mid sixties after all that gardening, gave a mighty heave and twisted herself away from Jarek. By doing so she lost her balance however and toppled over, sinking onto her hall carpet. The three crouched down beside her, now she was in a much easier position and Jarek could join in the feeding frenzy once again.

They had stopped laughing and now concentrated on their task in earnest, cramming and ramming pieces of paper into her mouth. There was little noise, only the gurgling and rasping of Mrs Webster as she attempted to rid herself of the wodges of pulp. The paper leaflets were bad enough but worst of all was the small cards, their sharp edges and shiny surfaces. She could no longer produce saliva; the only moisture in her mouth was blood from paper cuts and if she was going to try and swallow, this was no use as a lubricant.

A shadow appeared at the door.

Mr Sharma, Iracema and Jarek froze.

The man from Parcelforce rang the bell, and receiving no reply within the statuary wait of five seconds, scribbled the time of attempted delivery on a "While You Were Out" card which he pushed through the letter box before swiftly departing.

The trio had stopped in their tracks, papers poised, more shreds at the ready; six ears heard the rattle-slap of the letter box; six eyes watched the While You Were Out card hover, flutter, then land on the door mat. The shadow vanished from outside the door almost as quickly as it had appeared.

As they ignored Mrs Webster for a moment, she had the opportunity to raise herself up, and gagging and wheezing, she spat and removed paper from her mouth any way she could. She had seen the shadow at the door, though her eyes were streaming and had managed to croak, "Nnnngggghhhpppp..." for all the good it did her. The delivery man also had his MP3 player and heard only Coldplay. Jarek picked up the card from Parcelforce and added it to the feast, thereby ending Mrs Webster's brief moment of respite.

"Enough, I think, friends," said Mr Sharma at last. The spell was broken, their frenzy over. They had had their fun, such as it was. They stood over Mrs Webster as she rid herself of some last remnants of their flyers. She struggled for breath, turning ever redder in the face now that her ordeal was almost over. Iracema parcelled up the half chewed wads of paper into a flyer, and placed them in a side pocket of her satchel, tidying like the good cleaner she was. Likewise Mr Sharma and Jarek cleared away leaflets and cards that had been scattered around the hallway. You would hardly know they had been there. On an impulse Mr Sharma went to the front door, removed the hand-written card that said NO JUNK MAIL and looked at his companions, his head cocked to one side. He showed them the card, and raised a quizzical eyebrow in their direction.

"What do you think?" he asked.

Iracema stood over the woman who had made her cry. She nodded.

Jarek looked down at the woman with the filthy mouth. And because Iracema had nodded assent, Jarek did also. Mr Sharma, democratic to the last, tore the postcard into three, handed a piece to the girl, a piece to the other man, and as one they leaned over the woman and crammed the strips into her mouth. The card was thick, its edges were like tiny knives, and she had no saliva, no spittle left. Only the coppery gore.

And then they left.

Excelsior, HomeHelp and Rainbow went down the garden path, remembering to close the gate, and went their separate anonymous ways without a backward glance.

Mrs Webster flopped back on her hall carpet, gasping, choking. She could neither sit not raise herself up any more. The suddenness of their departure had taken her by shock, almost even greater than their arrival. She tried to roll on her side, she tried to retch, she tried to pull the pieces of card from her mouth but her assailants had rammed them far back, their parting gift to her. Her gorge rose, she managed to pull a small piece free, but the rest was blocking her airway, her fingers couldn't find a way to clear the sodden mass; she couldn't even spit the pieces out, some were becoming so saturated with her blood that small balls were detaching themselves and falling to the back of her throat, acting as a dam and restricting the air supply.

There was a tingling in her left arm, a sharp shock shot down through it, leaving her hand limp and useless. She was trapped on her back, aware only of the sensation of the tight band that the doctor warned her about and a stabbing in her chest worse than any knife. Was this how it was going to be? Without even the dignity of a clean and comfortable room in a hospice? No-one to tend her, to ease her final minutes? To clean away her final humiliation?

If only she could crawl through to the kitchen to her angina medication which was on the kitchen table.

If only.

ALL IN A ROW

London 1967

Janey was dazzling. Dominic was dazzled. Through the viewfinder she was a goddess, he couldn't make her more beautiful if he tried. Why would he want to? Flawless. Peerless. That skin, light, creamy, with just the hint of summer bronze. That hair, was it copper? Titian? Russet? He was an educated man but in her presence the words to describe her incomparable, matchless beauty failed him.

The client buzzed around his ears like a September wasp, sluggish yet dangerous. The studio was small, the client was not, and he was taking up to much space in his Dougie Millings suit and his Mr. Fish shirt.

"Get in there, Dominic, we want to show her eyes, we're selling fucking mascara here, not something from the fucking Uffizi." His wife had taken him there once. He knew Art.

But Janey. Those eyes, ah, those eyes. Sometimes navy blue, sometimes aquamarine, if the late afternoon sun caught her at a certain angle. Eyes that said come here. Eyes that said go away, you bore me. Eyes that said stay a while; stay forever if you want. I don't much care. Yes, those eyes.

Therefore mindful of the client's wish and the enormous pay day on offer, Dominic nodded to his assistant to move the lamps, to reposition Janey's chair so she could swivel, toss her hair, look deep into his lens and sell that fucking mascara.

"Nah," said the client. "More. Give me more. Get in close, Dominic. Get her to make love to the camera. It's what we're fucking paying you for."

He hovered and flapped at the periphery of Dominic's vision.

And so Dominic did. He got in close.

And Janey frowned, blinded and dazzled in her turn as she now was.

And the client's secretary chose that moment to re-enter the studio, having gone out to make a phone call.

And Dominic's assistant who was new to the job, had stretched the cable to its limit while repositioning the spot lamp to bring it close to Janey.

And the client's secretary was unaware of this and she tripped, fell and swore.

And the lamp also fell, exploding as it did so.

And Janey's face was pierced by a thousand pieces of glass.

Bissoe 1988

A long weekend away, head down to Cornwall in the car, stop off at some small bed & breakfast places; drive the country lanes, head to the north coast, wilder and less touristy than the south. That was the plan. Andrew had been working too hard, Anna was feeling neglected, and a few days away was something they both needed. And it seemed like a very good plan indeed. It would do them both the world of good and they would return to their small flat in Putney relaxed, refreshed, restored.

The rain had not helped. Cornish rain is much worse than London rain or Liverpool rain for when it falls it is often spoiling a holiday. It lingers and brings with it damp that stays like an unwelcome houseguest even when the rain has stopped. Their first choice of accommodation was closed until May, according to the hand written sign on the cottage door, and they had not been lucky with the random selections. Purple nylon sheets and streaky bacon were not conducive to a romantic break. Anna refused to share the driving except on the motorway as she hated the winding country roads. Too many tractors and not enough passing places. And Andrew had stopped once or twice, possibly even three times to phone the office, just to check everything was progressing in his absence. Restful? No.

They were on the outskirts of Truro, heading for a small hotel that had rooms available that night. Andrew learned this from a non-office related phone call. Anna was map reading. She had navigated the A39 easily enough, but the smaller roads were causing some confusion and something had gone wrong around Devoran. It had looked easy enough before they left Falmouth that morning.

They stopped at a crossroads and according to the sign the nearest village was called Bissoe.

Anna squinted through the dirty windscreen, and repeated the name over and over like a mantra.

"Bissoe, Bissoe, Bissoe..." She turned the map this way and that trying to locate the name, attempted to refold it and only succeeded in annoying Andrew.

"Chrissakes, Anna, give it up. I'll take this turning to bloody Bissoe wherever the hell it is and ask someone, or find a pub and use the phone."

"Don't snap at me, and can't you go one day without phoning your office. It is the weekend. They'd manage if you died you know." She thought at times like this, when he was frayed and scratchy, that she would too.

"I wasn't going to call the office. I was going to call this hotel to get directions, you stupid mare. Now lose that bloody map and let me see the road."

It was "stupid mare" that finally did it after a weekend of petty snipes and snaps; it was the notion that he could address her in that fashion, as if she, with her MA in the History of Art, was no more than a downtrodden housewife in an inferior television comedy.

Before he could make the turning, she thrust the crumpled road map at him, scooped up her bag from the floor, opened the passenger door and got out of the car, remembering to slam it behind her. He always hated that. Shouldering her bag, she set off in the opposite direction and marched down Bissoe Road away from the village. She might have known this if she'd held the road map the correct way up. Andrew watched his pretty young wife stride out in her silly city shoes and let her go. She was heart-breaking, funny, tender and deeply irritating. He was too tired after this allegedly relaxing weekend break to continue with the level of unpleasantness they had reached, and so he took the sign towards Bissoe and drove away from her. He'd give her a while to calm down then once those shoes began to hurt she'd be glad enough to see him when he eventually drew up alongside. Give her an hour or so maybe. Check into the Truro hotel then come back for her. That was his plan. She'd have calmed down by then, he'd be genial, reasonable and only tease her a little for her childish outburst. Yes, it would be fine. They'd salvage something from this break, somehow. Maybe even laugh about it with their friends back home in Putney.

"Go on sweetie, show them the shoes you were wearing," he'd say and she'd laugh and say, "Or what's left of them. My best Kurt Geiger's too!"

A solitary woman tended her front garden. It was set well back from Bissoe Road and over a mile from the village that consisted of a post office, a bus stop and little else. She was bent over a small plot of earth, scooping out soil, feeling her way round the hole and then locating a lobelia in early bud which she placed into it, packing earth around the small flowers. The planting was easy, the earth damp after a good night's soaking and the easy rhythm of the task pleased her: scoop, bed, pat, scoop, bed, pat, scoop, bed, pat. She had worked all morning without interruption and there was a sea of mixed lobelias swelling round her, in shades of pale blue and royal blue, the shades chosen specifically. The woman wore a large hat and sunglasses on this bright spring morning, and seemed dressed more appropriately for high summer than a good April day in Cornwall, where spring could often be fitful and reluctant to appear. Straightening up from her labours she turned her head slightly towards the road that was hidden from the property, distracted by the sound of strange footsteps approaching. They were not Dominic's, not the postman's, nor Miss Trethowan's from the nursery. These were city shoes, city footsteps, shoes with high heels, possibly sling backs, as she heard the crack-slap, crack-slap as they neared her. She knew about footwear. She turned back to her planting in the hope they might simply go away.

"Oh, thank Christ there's somebody here," said a strange voice. It was as unfamiliar to her as the footfall. It was a London accent, somewhere in the south east, not clipped or precise but certainly from one of the better suburbs.

"Sorry, sorry to trouble you, but do you think I could borrow your phone? I'm stuck, I mean, I don't have transport and I need to phone for a taxi, maybe get into Truro, catch a train, something like that."

Anna paused by a gate set into a high laurel hedge that opened on to a wonderful garden. She would have taken time to admire it had her feet not been in rebellion after walking for half an hour in her ridiculous shoes down a rutted country lane and dodging last night's puddles. The woman bent over her gardening might not have heard her, so she tried again, pitching it up.

"Hello? Er, hello. Look I say, I'm sorry to bother you but I wonder if you could help..."

The woman still didn't turn, but straightened her back. This was the only clue that she was aware of another's presence.

"There's no need to shout, I'm not deaf."

"Sorry," said Anna, daring to open the gate and step into the garden, rather than wait for an invitation. She wasn't prepared to surrender lightly the opportunity of escape she hoped this encounter might present.

"Yes, come in, why don't you?" The gardener stood at last, though still her back was towards Anna.

"Look, I really don't want to be a nuisance but do you mind if I borrow your phone. I need to call a taxi."

"Yeah, heard you the first time. I think our phone's dead. Sorry, can't help." The conversation was over as far as she was concerned, so the woman began a slow and measured walk up the garden path towards the front door, counting her steps. Anna risked further rejection by following, at which point the woman turned at last. Anna saw huge sunglasses, and badly dyed red hair partially obscured by a large sunhat. More alarmingly, what she could see of the face was badly scored and scarred. However, so determined was she to reach the nearest town, 'civilisation' as she was beginning to think of it, that she ploughed on regardless, hiding her slight discomfort at the sight.

"Okay, no phone. Right. Well, is there anyone near by? Someone with a car?"

Before the woman could answer or dismiss her again, a male voice, accompanied by the trill of a bicycle bell, said, "Darling, I'm back! Ah, I see we have a visitor! How fabulous."

Some small respite from the woman's hostility was welcome and Anna turned to see who had appeared.

The man parked his bike inside the gate. He was maybe early forties, had been handsome, even pretty perhaps a decade or two ago but now was running to plump around the jawline and the middle, with thinning hair that touched his shoulders.

He joined the woman, kissed her, then regarded Anna.

"And what brings you to these parts? Holiday? Lost are

you? I didn't see a car. Luggage?"

So much affability after the reception from his partner was something of a shock. Anna said, "Um yes, sort of a holiday but now I really need to get back to London. I thought if I could get to Truro I could catch a train. No, no car, no luggage. Bit of a long story that. I just came across your place and I wondered if I could phone for a cab, get into Truro. But your wife said the phone was out or something."

"Ah, did she now?"

"I'm sorry to be such a nuisance but I really do have to get into town. I don't suppose you could give me a lift?" Anna looked around for another means of transport, other than the elderly bike that now was propped in front of the garden gate.

"Sorry no, the jalopy's at the garage failing its MOT right now I shouldn't wonder. Hence the trusty steed." He indicated the bike and smiled with the merest shrug of apology. "Look, come in and we'll have a cuppa and see if we can't sort you out somehow."

Anna could have cried with relief.

"Oh thank you, thank you so much, Mr...?"

"I'm Dominic and this is my sweet Janey. Welcome to our humble home."

"Anna," she said extending her hand. He took it and held it in both his while he studied her, looked deep into her blue eyes.

"Anna. A lovely name. Isn't that a lovely name, darling?" Almost as an afterthought he turned to the woman in the hat, who kept her head down, hiding her face.

As Anna led the way up the garden path, after an operatic flourish from Dominic to indicate the way, she thought she heard the woman, Janey, ask him, "Is she pretty?" and then a murmur from him, followed by the woman saying, "Yes, thought so..." Despite the tepid reception, Anna was quietly delighted with the woman's response. It was the nearest thing to a compliment she had had for some while. She didn't catch the next comment though, as Dominic whispered into his wife's hair: "And that's good, my darling, very good indeed."

Inside the house, it was cool and slightly damp after a night's heavy rain. With Anna in the lead, the trio went through to the back into a large farmhouse kitchen, complete with cream Aga, flags on the floor and expensive terracotta tiles on the walls, from Casa Pupo if she was any judge. The kitchen cabinets looked hand built, there were beech worktops, an enormous butcher's block, and in the centre of the room was a large refectory table with bentwood chairs. It was the sort of kitchen that Anna and her friends in London SW5 dreamed of, because that season their hearts were set on rustique chic. She momentarily forgot the unpleasantness with Andrew and the fact that she was out in the wilds of Cornwall without any visible means of rescue, so taken was she with her surroundings. Wait until she told Sarah and the girls about this!

While Anna gazed in admiration and not a little envy, Janey headed straight out to the back through the kitchen's stable door. Dominic filled the kettle while Anna ran her hands lightly over the table, tracing its knots and scratches and history.

"So young lady, what brings you to our door? We don't get too many people just popping in you know, but we rather like it like that, set well back from prying eyes. Sometimes country folk can be a bit odd, not like us at all." He gave her a conspiratorial wink.

"I am so sorry, I don't want to be any bother but yours was the first place I came to. I've been walking for ages, well it seems like it, and I'm trying to get to Truro..."

"Yes, you already said that. Not really dressed for it, if you don't mind me saying!" He regarded her footwear.

"Um no, my trainers and stuff are – elsewhere." This

was no time for a confession and her answer hung in the air like damp laundry for a moment. Dominic busied himself with mug, boiling water, teabag, and added a splash of milk from a blue striped pitcher.

"Spot of bother on the old domestic front, am I right?"

Suddenly he was at her side with that cup of tea. He was very close, too close. She could see the enlarged pores on his nose and several days of stubble. Sweat patches showed under the arms of his denim shirt. Outdoors he had seemed warm and genial; indoors he presented something rather less appealing. Anna looked around; even the hostile Janey would be welcome now, another person to engage. She noticed the phone standing on a dresser.

"D'you think you could see if the phone's back on?"

"Oh, yes, we sometimes get cut off when the weather's bad. Awful last night, localised you know. Two miles down the road, dry as a bone! Anyway, let's just see if we're in luck shall we?"

He went to the dresser, raised the handset with his back to her and unplugged the phone in one swift motion, dropping the cable end out of sight. He turned, apologetic once more and held out the handset for her to witness the silence.

"See? Sorry, dead as a dodo. Tell you what, you take your cuppa outside and have a little chat with Janey while I bike over to a mate's and see if he's any better off. They seem to be with a different exchange or something. Then I'll call the local cab firm from his. How does that sound?"

"Sounds good to me," said Anna. Glad of an escape, but desperate not to offend in case he was yet to be her salvation, she smiled at him. Then she went out through the stable doors, though she somehow doubted that a 'little chat' with Janey was a likely option.

The land behind the property was completely different to the front, which was all lawn and flowerbeds, a true cottage garden. Anna discovered at the back something more like an allotment. There was one raised bed of planting, but other beds were full of vegetables, of broccoli and leeks. Had she been less of a city girl she would have also recognised chard, rocket and mizuna. A large greenhouse and two sheds, much larger than anything her father had in his garden in Mortlake, were behind these beds and everything was enclosed by a low wall. Beyond this there was a muddy field with pigs, some with their young.

Anna, ever the curious townie, was drawn by their squeals and would have risked her shoes further to have a look, but thought she had better attempt a conversation with this strange, uncommunicative woman in the large hat. Besides her husband had gone to try and muster a cab for her, hadn't he, so it wasn't all bad.

The woman was tending the raised bed of plants and she seemed to be feeling her way along it. Once again her back stiffened as she sensed the presence of the younger woman.

"Your phone's still out I'm afraid. Your husband's offered to go to a friend's place, see if theirs is working."

"Has he now?" said Janey, apparently uninterested. The smallest smile reached her lips however.

Try another tack, reasoned Anna. This little nightmare could be over in half an hour if I get lucky. I could be away from this rather odd couple and heading off towards civilization.

"It's a fascinating place you've got here. Do you grow your own stuff?"

"Some."

"I suppose you'd call it a smallholding, would you?"

"I suppose."

"A bit like Tom and Barbara in *The Good Life* then?" The joke was feeble but worth a go.

"The good life?"

"Yes, you know, that thing on the TV. Well, it used to

be. Ages ago. Richard Briers and Paul Something-or-other. They're always showing repeats."

Janey turned towards Anna.

"I haven't watched TV in a very long time," she said. She removed her sunglasses, revealing a face that was scarred and rutted beyond repair; one eye was closed up, the socket completely puckered, while the other eye had a milky opalescent hue, like a cheap marble. The absolute shock of the other woman's stripped face now exposed, threatened to unhinge Anna. This was turning out to be a day of too many surprises.

"What the...? Oh, fuck," she said. "I'm sorry, I didn't realise... I...Oh, shit...You poor thing!" she shrugged helplessly. "I really didn't have a clue."

"Why should you?"

"No, I know but, oh shit..."

"Shhhh, now," Janey said, strangely soothing. "Come here, come over here to me."

Anna, stricken and embarrassed, yet calmed by the change in her tone, did as she was told; she walked towards the blind woman, hypnotised by that mess of a face. Janey stretched out her hands and felt Anna's soft young firm skin; she traced fingers across the fine contours of her cheekbones and chin, and over her well formed eyebrows and round her lovely full lips. For a moment as they continued their journey round Anna's face, they strayed horribly close to her eye sockets. Her fingers were covered in damp soil and she left black smears on the younger woman's cheeks as she explored her perfection. Anna, desperate for distraction, looked over Janey's shoulder at the area where she'd been working. A trowel lay beside a recently prepared hole that was maybe five inches deep, and about ten inches round. It was at the end of a row of what appeared to be intricate floral displays, each one roughly the size and shape of a large cabbage. They were all different colours, some pale, some creamy coloured, one or two very rosy indeed. One was a light brown. On closer inspection the displays also seemed to have eyes, noses and mouths, though Anna with her ignorance of all things horticultural couldn't make out what they had been grown from. Had Janey added small vegetables or tiny plants to create the impression of human features? If so, she was very skilled for a blind woman. Then she looked harder at the row and realised that they were not constructed from an artful arrangement of plants at all.

She realised that she was looking at a row of heads.

Were they dolls' heads then?

Anna saw that these were larger, more life like.

No, they weren't dolls.

Each of the heads was a girl's face, a pretty young face, and each, even the brown one, had blue eyes; some sapphire coloured, some azure, one the colour almost of lapis lazuli, but all had blue, blue eyes. They sparkled like glass.

"Sweet God in heaven. What are they?" she whispered. "Waxworks?"

"Did you hear that, Dom? She wants to know if they're waxworks." Janey actually laughed, she threw back her head and laughed.

"So shall we add her to your collection then, my darling?" asked her husband.

"Oh yes. You must. This one is pretty, very pretty indeed."

Dominic had not pedalled to his friend's house, for he had no friends in the locale. He had ventured no further than the back door where he kept a woodsman's axe perfectly honed for an occasion such as this.

Anna turned at the sound of his voice. Janey moved to one side so as not to impede his progress and in one swift and practised movement Dominic brought the axe down onto Anna's neck, thereby separating that very pretty head from her slender shoulders in a stroke. Whether they were standing or bending or even kneeling, it made no difference to him. He could take them any way. He was awfully good. Of course there was that one girl who had been lying down, sunbathing on the front lawn. She had turned as his shadow fell over her, axe poised for the strike. With the momentum he had followed through and embedded his blade in the grass. Rapid action and a couple, well four, messy strokes had saved the day. But she was one of the earlier ones. Now he was a master, as adept as any executioner in Tudor England.

"There, darling, another one for you!" he scooped up Anna's head by her flowing blonde locks and her body crumpled onto the garden path which was soon made treacherous by gouts of pumping blood.

"Well done, my clever, clever Dominic."

Janey almost swooned with delight as the coppery scent reached her nostrils, for her sense of smell equalled her sense of hearing. "There's a spot all ready for her," she said.

"I'll start on her straight away, brain and tongue tonight, then begin the treatment," her husband said.

"And the eyes, don't forget the eyes," Janey sounded almost nervous.

"How could I forget the most important part? What shade would you like for this one?"

"What colour is her hair?"

"She's blonde. Natural too," he said admiring the dripping head and examining the parting in her hair. Anna's torso lay crumpled and ignored on the path.

"Then a light blue, I think. Yes, light blue. Nordic."

"Just like her real colour in fact," he said as he raised head to eye level and checked her orbs, wide open and innocent. "Nordic Anna. A perfect choice!" He tried to congratulate Janey with a kiss but she drew away. He would kill for a kiss from his lovely wife.

"Is there enough wax?"

Dominic ran his free hand over those torn features to

soothe her. Dear, dear Janey, forever his beautiful Janey. It was always the same: her initial ecstasy with each new trophy was followed by anxiety, but she was calm and tranquil again once a new head was added to her collection.

"Darling pet lamb, don't worry. Yes, there's wax. Just go inside. Go and rest, my love. I'll help you, we don't want you slipping in the blood now, do we?"

And so with the head of one lady in his left hand and holding his wife with the other he guided her back towards the safety of the kitchen while the blood continued to spread down the path.

Indoors Janey felt her way through the kitchen towards the hall and the staircase. She counted up the twenty-three stairs, turned right at the top and went into her bedroom. She would let Dominic join her here later as a reward for today's prize. She would tolerate his stale breath and his rough skin and his sweat; she would even endure his endless moaning, his sighs of gratitude. He earned these little treats from time to time, sometimes as many as four a year, as his mastery in the arts of decapitation and embalming flourished. From the first one, many years ago, whom he had bludgeoned with a cricket bat and wasn't really worth the saving, to the last eight which were works of art. She couldn't see them but she could feel them, feel their lovely features, smooth and regular. There was nothing to mar their perfection. Ever.

And their pigs, their lovely little rare breed pigs, would prosper and fatten and grow as they fed on the girls' other body parts. And their bones would be ground down in one of the sheds to be used as fertiliser. Nothing was wasted.

And then a farmer from nearby would collect the porkers, and he would take them to be butchered, returning with them in manageable joints, which they would store in an industrial sized freezer in the other shed.

And she and Dominic would feast on them.

And on the Bissoe Road, Andrew drove past the house

six times, unaware of its existence behind the high laurel hedge.

Where was the silly bitch? He thought he should have caught up with her by now.

DAD DANCING

Aren't parents embarrassing when they dance? Especially dads. It's that sideways shuffle they do, with elbows at the sides and feet slithering. Sometimes they click their fingers too. It's not really dancing; with heads flung back, they move to a private rhythm that has nothing to do with the music, the sounds from their youth: The Beatles, (not bad); Boney M, (don't go there); The Bee Gees, (unbefuckinlievable). The slither thing is bad enough, but worse is the disco dance, which is beyond gross. For that one they sort of twist on the balls of the feet, one arm up, one down, or spin slowly pointing at whoever gets into their eye line. Look at me; I am s-o-o-o-o-o dangerous. There's really nothing dangerous about a middle-aged man wearing new jeans with a crease ironed in, and a fancy shirt revealing a gold chain nestling in damp, matted chest hair. However otherwise jovial, generous or charming the parent, it is something no child should ever have to witness.

Twins Nic and Anton were cursed with such a parent. For the first ten years of their lives it was less of an issue, though even from a relatively tender age they felt there was something just not *right* about such displays. They had been christened respectively Nicholas and Anthony by their mother, and were called Nicky and Tony by their father. The sobriquets Nic and Anton were of their own choosing. Now well into their seventeenth year, they were armed with the vocabulary to give voice to their discomfort. Of an age when poise and style were paramount, their millionaire father from Peckham let them down in so many ways. It wasn't just the dancing; it wasn't just the gold chains and the sovereign rings and the glittering diamond in one ear.

This last was a six-month anniversary present from wife number two, Staci. It wasn't just the accent, which marked him out as the son of a South London costermonger. No, also to be taken into consideration was his height. And his weight. Even his name: Ron. Not Ronald, not even Ronnie, but Ron. One syllable, three letters, no embellishment, nothing. Ron. But mainly it was the dancing.

The boys were not effete, not by a long stretch; they played rugby and cricket for their overpriced school in Berkshire, climbed and skied in Scotland, and with their fellows chased the pretty village maidens who they gamely referred to as "tarts." They were growing into perfect specimens of manhood. For the past two years they had enjoyed the hospitality of their peers during Easter and summers vacs. While dad went to his whitewashed villa with wrap-around sun terraces on a golf course in Mar-bay-ah, the boys headed to the Highlands or the Vendee. There they would dress in faded shorts and old-fashioned rugby jerseys with the collars turned up, lingering in the company of fragrant virgins called India and Kitty, Flora and Hermione. When they returned from the first such excursion, nothing back at home was ever quite the same again. Their father, who had amassed his not incon-siderable pile through plumbing supplies, was frankly appalled when they told him how the hot water packed up at the Hon. Angus's parent's place, as it so often did. And then there were the high flush toilet cisterns, with bits of old rope attached to the pulling mechanism!

"Bit of a hoot, really," they said, echoing Angus.

"Nah. You should bring some of yer mates here, let them see some decent plumbing, proper karseys," he had offered.

He was justifiably proud of the five-bed-five-bath house, a symbol of his upward mobility from Peckham to the leafy acres of Wimbledon Common. Each en suite was a different colour: peach, champagne, sea mist, eau de nil, sun blush. All very tasteful, very classy, and chosen by Staci after consultation with the developer.

"Mmm," said Anton.

"Yah, right," said Nic.

Christmas was looming. Before the twins were able to go and frolic on the ski slopes with India, Angus, and the gang, there was the small matter of the festivities to be endured. The Christmas period itself was bad enough with relatives descending on them, but at least there was some perverse fun to be picked from the carnage, and Dad's legendary generosity also helped. The real problem was New Year, more specifically, New Years Eve. A big party. Catering. Live music. Karaoke. And dancing. Lots and lots of it.

Anton said, "The thought of it, Nic..."

"Simply chills the blood," finished his brother, the older by six minutes.

Some weeks previously they had tried to negotiate a peaceful withdrawal from the end of year revelries.

"Thing is, Dad, some of the gang will be heading up to Aviemore after Christmas. Ruairidh's people have a place. They'd love us to join them."

The reality was that an invitation was yet to be forthcoming, but the twins would worry about that at a later date. The priority was to avoid another ghastly New Year's Eve with Ron.

"I daresay they would, Nicky. I don't doubt it. However I want my boys here for New Year. We'll have everyone round, just like we've always done. They all talk about it for weeks afterwards, and it wouldn't be the same without my boys."

Here the proud pater familias stretched up and clapped an arm round each of them, the fruit of his loins. He slapped their backs with an enthusiasm which neither son felt the occasion merited.

"Tell yer what, get yer mates to come here, Roar-ree and Anus and all the rest of 'em."

His sons chose to ignore the charmless pun on their friend's name.

"Plenty of room for everyone. Whaddaya say?"

He beamed up at them, turning his head from one boy to the other, his small brown eyes twinkling with the excitement of it all.

Nic paled. Some time ago he and Anton had made an unofficial pact that none of their friends could ever cross the threshold of the family home. Not one. Never. It would be a slow and painful social death.

"Don't think so, Dad," he said.

"No," added Anton. "They've made their plans. It's a..."

"Family tradition thing. They go straight up there..."

"Right after Christmas every year," finished the younger boy, honing the lie.

They hoped Dad would empathise with the notion of family + tradition as it was close to his heart. They were to be disappointed.

"Well, never mind, eh. You can go and join 'em after New Year's Day."

Nic made a last effort, a reckless bid for freedom.

"Yah, but we sort of told them we'd join them before Hogmanay..."

"Hogmanay schmogmanay, you stay here."

"But it'd be rude not to keep our word," said Anton.

Ron's currant sized eyes glittered and turned as black as coals. He removed his hands from the boys' backs and walked around them, rubbing a hand over his cropped bullet head.

"They're rather expecting us," continued Anton.

Their father rounded on them, faster than a bull turning into the matador's cape.

"Fuckin' 'ell," he said. "What have I spent on your

education? What part of 'no' don't you get? N – O equals no. No. Got that?"

A stubby forefinger waggled under each nose, as Ron spun from Anton to Nic, then back again.

Nic towered over his father by some six inches and opened his mouth for one final attempt.

"But we told them..."

He got no further. Ron drew back his hand with the be-ringed fingers and slapped the face of his first-born. A pistol crack, a stinging, then it was over. Nic stood his ground and did not even touch the smarting cheek nor staunch the trickle of blood. As his face reddened with the blow, his father's was wreathed in smiles once more.

"Right, now we got that sorted. Good boys, good boys. We'll have a laugh, few bevvies, bit of a dance. Just like we always do," he said, treating them to a twirl in the manner of an overweight middle-aged Greek gigolo. He clapped his hands together, rubbing them with unbridled joy.

"Yeah, just like we always do."

The incident was not referred to again, and Nic and Anton chose not to speak of it when alone together. There was no need. Ruairidh's people eventually issued an invitation, and so with Ron's benediction, the brothers made plans to join their friends in Scotland early in the New Year for some skiing once the public transport system was accessible again. Next year there was the promise of seventeenth birthdays and driving tests and cars, which assuaged the disappointment somewhat. But only somewhat.

Christmas Day came and with it some spinster aunts and Staci's aged parents, who bought a giant jigsaw puzzle for the boys. Nic and Anton managed to smile and permit furry kisses from the old girls and bore it all with a stoicism that is only found in teenagers who have been given very large cheques to spend at will.

December 30th saw the house a hive of activity as a small army of party planners took up occupation in preparation for the event the following evening. Staci didn't want to wear herself out as she said it might bring on 'one of my 'eads,' but anyway Ron was happy to hand over management to a team of well drilled and highly paid professionals.

His theme, according to the printed invitations, was 'Saturday Nite (sic) Feeva (sic)' and guests were expected to arrive suitably attired. He had opted for a white suit with waistcoat, and a black satin shirt. In anticipation of the night to come, his mood brightened while that of his sons' darkened. The vast array of cheques, Christmas socks and jigsaw puzzles gathered dust in their respective bedrooms, overlooked and ignored, as their loathing for the forthcoming event grew and grew. With every chair that was moved, every glass that was polished they flinched anew. The ceremonial installation of the glitter ball in the conservatory was the final straw.

"It's like being crucified," moaned Anton.

"Yah, like the nails going in," agreed Nic.

"It's horrible, too horrible..."

"...to contemplate. He and Barbi are having a dress rehearsal."

That was their private name for Staci. Her similarity to the plastic toy with the pneumatic body and overly large blonde hair was not lost on them.

"Trying on their disco king and queen outfits? Oh God no. I don't think..."

"...I can stand much more."

"No, me neither."

"If only..." said Nic.

"Yes, if only..." said Anton.

They sighed in tandem.

Anton looked at Nic. Nic looked at Anton. They had inherited their mother's very pale blue eyes and dark brown hair, plus her slender build and height.

As each boy gazed deep into his twin's pair of icy orbs, words were no longer necessary for empathy was total. Their mother had died when they were eight and it was a capacity they discovered within themselves from that time onwards. Their father found their silent communication unnerving to say the least, that and the tendency to finish each other's sentences. Staci agreed with her husband, it was downright creepy. In fact, she privately thought they were a pair of insufferable little snots, with their posh airs and their rugby matches, smelly, cracked old Barbour jackets, and skiing trips, and friends who spelled their names all wrong. I mean, Rory was spelled R-O-R-Y for God's sake, not Ruairidh.

Anton went to his father's room, the room with the super-king-sized bed, where Staci would join him on occasion. Birthdays, anniversaries, good wins for Chelsea, that sort of thing. The arrangement between husband and wife worked well enough, though she preferred to wait for the bruises to heal between visits.

Ron was standing in front of a full-length mirror in his dressing room, posing in the white suit and black shirt. The jacket was hooked over one finger and slung carelessly over his shoulder. He seemed strangely unembarrassed at being discovered thus, and unless he had lost weight in the week since Christmas, the only other possible explanation was that he was wearing a corset.

His second born was almost lost for words.

"Wow," he managed.

"Waddya think? Yer old man still got it then? Eh?"

His father came at him, aimed a jocular punch at his son's upper torso in the way so beloved of men of a certain age. He exuded bonhomie from every pore.

"Goodness," said Anton. He smiled.

"What you two rascals up to then? Getting yerselves something fancy sorted for tomorrow night? Something to get the girls goin' then, eh?"

This was accompanied by a nifty bit of footwork and a swift one-two jab-jab at Anton's body.

If he touches me once more I might just break his back, thought the boy. He was capable.

"Well yes, we're working on something. Something a bit special."

He only avoided the two playful taps his father was about to place on both his cheeks by sidestepping a little and pretending to arrange his fringe in the mirror.

"Brilliant! Bleedin' marvellous!"

"Pleased?"

"'Course I am. My two boys! Who wouldn't be?"

Anton took the plunge.

"So well, all that unpleasantness before, when we said we wanted to go to Scotland straight after Christmas...?"

He let the question hang. He knew his father would pounce on it.

"Nah. All forgotten. Me and my boys, that's what counts."

Ron looked ready to split in two; he was beaming harder than seemed possible. And was that a glint of something moist in his eyes? His lovely boys were planning something special for New Years Eve, and it was all for him! Blessed, that's what he was. Blessed.

Anton sighed, suddenly downcast despite this tender rapprochement.

"Thing is, Dad..."

"Woss up, son? Woss wrong?"

"Thing is, Nic's a bit, well, he's still a bit hurt by um, what happened then. The slap thing? I know we had a great Christmas and all that, but you know how he takes things to heart, and well..."

He trailed off, leaving his father to ponder a while.

Having given him time to consider, he then applied his masterstroke.

"Dad, could you, would you tell him you're sorry? You don't even need to say it to his face. You could write it. Just let him know you're sorry. Then we can all start afresh. New year, new start, all that?"

Ron looked up at his younger son, in some ways so much the wiser than his sibling.

"Nicky put you up to this, 'as he?"

"Oh Lord, no. He'd be really hacked off if he knew..."

Anton smiled, a picture of innocence, and tossed his fringe out of his eyes to gauge his father's response.

Ron went to his bureau, took a blank piece of paper, wrote just one word on it and signed it. He folded it over, handed it to the boy and said,

"Garn, now get outta here."

As Anton left his father's room and walked the length of the upper landing towards his brother's, he heard the dreaded opening bars of 'Stayin' Alive' and his father joining in with the lyrics.

Some hours later the house, decked in all its seasonal finery, was in darkness. Staci slept in her own room, as she didn't feel strong enough for a visit with her husband just yet. She couldn't leave it too long though. Due gratitude must be shown for the Lexus. Ron slumbered in the master suite while frost twinkled on the stone lions at the gateposts.

The house held its breath for the excitement that was to come.

A figure crept into Ron's room; a shadow stole across the carpet and leaned over the hillock in the bed that was his body. Somewhere a clock struck three and the only other sounds were his own measured breathing, and the slightly shorter breaths of the intruder.

A hand reached out, touched the sleeping man on the

shoulder, then shook him. Struggling with the duvet, he fought his way to consciousness, angered at the invasion of his domain.

"Whatthefucksgoinon?"

Anton revealed himself.

"Shhh, Dad. It's only me."

"Tony?"

"Dad, you need to come downstairs. I think there's someone in the garage. I couldn't sleep and I thought I heard something. I went into Nic's room, and he's gone down already."

Ron shot out of bed, and for a big man could move with some speed when stirred. Without even bothering to get slippers or robe – no need as there was under-floor heating, and the house was kept at a constant temperature throughout the night – he hurried past his son, out onto the landing and down the curved staircase. He didn't stop to consider how his younger boy might have heard noises travel all the way from the downstairs garage area to the bedrooms on the upper floor, but logic did not dictate his reactions. Concern for his Aston Martin and for Staci's Lexus did.

"Those fuckin caterers, they've been sniffing round all day. I bet one of them's behind it. Cunts. Woss Nicky gone down there for? Fuckin idiot. He could get his head stove in."

With Anton hard on his heels he went through a connecting door from the hallway to the garage, which was in darkness. Ron slapped the switch, once, twice, nothing happened. Unbeknown to him, the overhead light bulbs had been loosened some moments before. He heard a movement and saw a figure beside his Aston Martin, bending over the windscreen.

"Oi you, just fucking stop right there. Tony, go and phone the rozzers." He couldn't help himself, he often spoke like a character from a second-rate television drama.

Anton stayed put.

In the murkiness of the garage, the only faint light was from the buffed bodywork of a quarter of a million pounds worth of motorcars. As his eyes grew accustomed to the gloom the figure propped against his prize car began to take on a more familiar aspect.

"Nicky? That you?"

"Yah. 'S me."

Ron stumbled over to him. "Where'd the fuckers go?"

He slept in brown silk pyjamas with his initials on the pocket and presented no immediate threat. How the 'burglars' would have laughed!

"Panic over, there was nobody here after all," said Nic, lounging on the car's bonnet. "Must have..."

"Imagined it," added Anton, joining him at the car.

Ron leaned over, his hands on his knees, as if he had been running and needed to catch his breath.

"Thank Christ for that. Fuck me. Coulda been nasty."

"Could have," agreed Nic.

"Very," said Anton.

"Still could," said Nic, for his brother's ears only.

"Mmmm," said Anton.

Their father rose to his full five feet and five inches.

"Right. Well then, get away from the car, and let's go back to bed."

Neither son moved.

"I said, get away..."

"From the car. Yah, heard you," said Nic.

Until the night's act of assumed, if thwarted, heroism, the boys had been banned from the garage for the past three years since one of them – he never knew which – had scratched that season's Ferrari with careless parking of a bike. Their bicycles from that day forth were left in a specially constructed shed.

Suddenly and swiftly, working as one and with no prompting, Nic and Anton, graceful as black cats, moved towards Ron. They pounced. His feet left the ground as he was lifted onto a footstool, barely thirty centimetres high. Anton wrapped him in an embrace that was designed purely to pinion his arms at his sides and confound his struggles.

"Whoa," he said.

"Shut up," Nic said.

Before he was able to make another comment, he found something slipped over his head and tightened round his neck; it felt coarse and constricted his breathing immediately. It was jerked sharply by Nic who had moved behind him and as he struggled, he looked up and saw that it was in fact a length of rope that had been coiled over a roof beam. His head was inside a noose. The rope dug deep into his neck, and his face began to swell, though due to lack of light it was not possible to fully appreciate the colour it was turning. In rapid succession it went from carmine to burgundy to the yellowish purple of an old bruise. Anton released his arms and he stood precariously on the stool, wobbling, thrashing and turning, fully awake at last. Speech was not possible, only wheezing, and a bubble of blood trickled down from his nose to be absorbed by the silk pyjama top. His chubby fingers went to the rope, though there was no slackening of it, no loosening, no give, as the strong young man behind him applied all his own weight to the job in hand. Turning once too often, Ron lost his footing and the stool slipped from beneath him. He was gurgling and choking, spitting and sighing, dying at the end of a piece of rope. Never a pretty man in life, in death he was an obscene caricature of the hanged man: deep plum face, bug eyes ready to pop from their sockets, and a bloated fat grey worm of a tongue protruding from liver coloured lips. His arms fell to his sides, fingers spasmed like sausages on a griddle; his legs kicked, while his feet continued to describe invisible steps in the air. A pool of urine formed just ten centimetres beneath his feet and steamed lightly on the cool floor.

Anton recorded the whole thing on his iPhone 7, newly purchased with a Christmas cheque.

"Oh look, Nic. Dad dancing!"

The older twin came round to inspect his handiwork and watched the instant replay on the phone.

"Bloody good show."

Content with their night's work, they tightened the light bulbs in the sockets, removed their latex surgical gloves, and retired to their respective bedrooms.

On the windscreen of the Aston Martin was a folded piece of paper. On it, written unmistakably in Ron's own hand were just two words: Sorry, Dad.

THE WAY AND THE TRUTH AND THE LIFE

John sank back in his chair, ecstatic and spent, as the boy left the room shutting the door between them. On the other side of that closed door he could not see the child's broken face as it crumpled, nor see him wipe the snot that flowed from his nostrils. The boy wanted to gag, to bring up the foul stuff. He prayed for water and scrubbed at his mouth trying to eradicate the taste. It would be with him for some time yet, and as a grown man he would be unable to eat certain shellfish for the remembrance that they brought with their salt tang. He wanted to run back into the room and quiz the man. Why me, he would say, what have I done? Sure, he'd been caught smoking, not that he was alone. And if he was often slow with the chores, did his punishment have to be this? He heard footsteps, accompanied by the soft clink-swing of rosary beads worn on a belt. Sister Aloysius was making the rounds on her weekly visit, and if he didn't make it back to the study room he'd be in for another reprimand, except here they called it 'correction.' The swipe of her broad strong hand across his face was preferable to swallowing Father John's jiz, but he made good his escape nonetheless.

Thirty years and four parishes later, Father John Ahern was alone in the kitchen of the priests' house. Father Malachy Flynn was visiting the hospice and Father Paul Horgan was taking his driving test for the fourth time. It was the housekeeper's day off, away to visit her widowed sister in Rathmines; two buses and a good walk, but she'd offer it up for her sins and the Holy Souls. On the threshold of his

71

eighth decade he still marvelled at the simplicity of folk, their plain honest beliefs and some might say their gullibility. A man of ferocious beliefs himself, in their gullibility lay his power.

He was making tea for the two gentleman visitors who sat in the front parlour, a cold space reserved for unwanted callers. John and the other priests preferred the small sitting room near the kitchen, where they could rant at the telly, smoke themselves up a grand old fug and enjoy a wee Jameson.

However back to the callers. He knew one of them, Michael O'Driscoll; he'd baptised him and his two sisters, and had officiated when Kathleen married that waster six years ago. He did not know the second one however, the one who showed his ID at the door while Michael hovered at his elbow. Edmund Leahy, it read. A Garda inspector.

"We'd like you to cast your mind back, when you were at St Francis Xavier's in Drumcondra. We understand you were there in the '70's. I have photographs of some of the boys who were in your charge," he'd said, without so much as a by-your-leave. The arrogant little bollocks.

At which point John announced he'd go and make the gentlemen a cup of tea, bound to be thirsty work all that talking, and he'd be only a minute or two. He left them huddled inside their overcoats in the parlour with a crucifix and a framed print of Christ's Committal to the tomb for company. He sensed what they were after, he wasn't stupid; there had been rumours. He poured three mugs of tea, reserving the chipped one for Inspector Leahy and spat into it, before giving it a final stir.

Carrying the mugs on a tin tray he contrived to slop some as he made his way back to the parlour. He knew their game, and shame on the O'Driscoll boy for being party to it. They'd have their work cut out trying to lay anything at his door.

"Right so, here you go, lads," he said, and Michael leapt

to his feet to assist. He'd been an altar boy, but then hadn't they all, a chubby little ginger-haired lad, not to John's liking at all. He'd always had a fondness for lean, dark-haired boys with blue eyes, classic Celtic looks. All that had been some time ago, and since then the slate had been clean. Of course there had been his visit to London a few years back, though that didn't matter, it was too far from home. He angled the tray so that Leahy received the chipped mug, and Michael the one with roses; his own was the Manchester United one, from the great days when Roy Keane played for them. Now there was a looker.

"Right so, what can I do for you fellas? Something about my days at St Francis Xavier's, you said?"

Edmund Leahy warmed his hands around the mug, which looked none too clean, and indicated the small selection of photographs that he'd spread out on the carpet. Some of them dated back more than thirty years, others were more recent. Michael O'Driscoll looked around the room, inspected his fingernails, his shoes, a loose thread on his sleeve; he looked anywhere except at the seventy-year old priest who had heard his confession, from whom he had received his First Holy Communion, and for whom he had served at Mass.

"Christ, do I have to go along?" he'd said back at the station. "Can't you take Byrne or O'Hanlon? I'm known to Father Ahern, it doesn't seem right."

"You're coming, and that's it. The fact that he knows you, knew you when you were little, it might unsettle him. I'm going to get that evil old fecker. We'll nail him, then just think how it'll look on your record. You'll be a hero. So get those snaps and let's go."

Leahy was small, dynamic and powerful, built like a scrum half, and the matter was not open to further discussion, even if O'Driscoll was related on his mother's side to the Divisional Officer.

"Do you recognise any of these boys, Father? They were

at St Francis Xavier's the time you were. Of course I do realise it's almost thirty years. I wonder if this face rings any bells for instance?"

He pointed to a photo taken in the early 1970's, a curly haired boy called Andrew Tolan. Most of the older photos were from one source, the man who had originally brought the case to the attention of the Gards, even though his approaches to the powers that be had been met with incredulity some twenty years before. Two decades on, and those same issues were now a matter of growing concern, for this time the Gards approached him. Leahy remembered his first meeting with the fellow, a forty-two year old man weeping like a woman as he told his story, exposing suppurating sores that had never healed. Probably never would. A thirty year old secret is hard to bear and harder to share.

Leahy watched Ahern as he received the photo, the slight shake in the hand, which was at odds with the man's physical bearing. When he had opened the door to himself and O'Driscoll, Leahy was taken by the man's strong good looks, a vigorous build, and a fine head of hair that was still predominantly brown. The reason for their visit briefly explained, the priest had ushered them into this ice-box of a room and then vanished to make tea. When he re-entered their presence he had developed a stoop and was faltering. A fine trick. Leahy put down his mug, and caught a small look of something in the priest's eyes, as he selected two more photographs for consideration. One of them was of the forty-two year old as a smiling boy of twelve, though God knows what he'd found to smile about, incarcerated in that hellhole called St Francis Xavier's. This industrial school for wayward or orphaned boys, was established in 1938 and run under the auspices of the Catholic Church and it had initially been a worthwhile institution. All that gradually changed and stories were now circulating of systematic and unparalleled sexual and mental abuse from the 1950's until 1982, the year it closed. This closure was not due to investigations by the Catholic Church hierarchy or the Gards, but because of a fire.

Ahern appeared to study the photos, then shook his head.

"It's hard to tell, Inspector. I need to find my spectacles, my eyesight's not what it was."

Leahy thought, oh God, not that old chestnut. Father Ahern was not the first priest he had had to visit regarding this ongoing enquiry, and it was interesting the amount of them who pleaded poor eyesight and had to go in search of their glasses. It gave them thinking time, to work out whatever lies they might need to tell. In this priest's case, he had been able to read the warrant card without their assistance. As he made to rise from his chair, Michael O'Driscoll pointed to a tortoiseshell frame that poked out from his top pocket.

"Isn't that them, Father?" he asked. Leahy silently blessed him.

"Ah, well spotted. Saved my poor old legs," said Ahern as he put them on. "Thank you, Michael. Or should I be calling you Garda O'Driscoll?"

Jesus H, we've gone from 'lads' to 'fellas' to 'Inspector' and 'Garda' in less than ten minutes, thought Leahy. He was keen to be getting along.

"Right, Father, if you could just take a moment or two to look at these photos, tell us who you recognise. Tell us anything you can about the lads in question."

John Ahern pursed his lips, scratched at his chin. He'd played the shaky-hands card, and the can't-see-too-well-without-my-glasses number, yet he still had a trick or two to stall these two.

"They were at St Francis Xavier's you say? Thirty years ago? Lots of boys came into our care then, it's difficult to remember. My memory's not what it used to be. I'm not a young man any more."

He handed the pictures back to Leahy, adding a small tremor for effect.

"And of course most of the boys were a bad lot, you know. Thievery, all sorts of shenanigans. Right little delinquents we had then. Culchies, many of them. Knackers, if you like. Bad blood. Uncontrollable. It's easier to recall the good boys that you come across, fellows like young Michael here."

O'Driscoll squirmed under his former parish priest's approbation, and sought distraction in his cooling tea.

"Uncontrollable, you say?" asked Leahy.

"Uncontrollable," repeated Ahern. He looked at Leahy. Conversation closed. "You've not touched your tea, Inspector."

"No, Father, I'm more of a coffee man, but thanks anyway."

He gathered up the photographs of boys: happy, frowning, smiling, scowling, laughing, sulking, cheering, shouting boys, and put them back in the folder where they were together in the dark once more. Had they ever sought comfort from one another at St Francis Xavier's? He suspected not. Back then none of them dared speak of the abuse that was their lot. Each victim he had recently interviewed had been adamant that the shame was too great, why share it with their peers? Each one assumed he and he alone had been singled out. He wondered if Andrew Tolan's suicide might have been avoided if he'd spoken to the other broken boys back then. Whatever.

The three men rose. Ahern held onto the chair arms for that extra bit of support, and then straightened up.

"I'm sorry I've not been much help. You fellows must think you've had a wasted journey."

Don't you believe it, pal, thought Leahy. "Sorry for taking up your time, Father. It was a bit of a long shot, we know that now."

"What is it exactly you do? Why do these boys need

investigating now?"

"Didn't I say? Sure, I'd forget my own head if it wasn't screwed on. We're not investigating the boys, Father. They've done nothing. We're with the Sexual Assault Investigation Unit, and we're currently examining accusations of abuse that may have taken place in religious institutions, as far back as the 1950's, though certainly from the 1970's."

Without blinking Ahern said, "Didn't I tell you, they were delinquents these boys, up to all sorts. But I'd no idea they were depraved too. Unnatural. God bless us and save us." He paused to make the Sign of the Cross to reassert his impeccable credentials, then sighed like his poor old heart might break. "And there we were trying to help them along, get them a decent start in life. It's too terrible to even think about, Inspector." He shook his leonine head at the horror of it all.

"It is indeed, Father," said Leahy. "Too terrible to think about." Christ, you're good, you evil old bastard. But I'm better.

Ahern was shepherding them to the front door. It was a raw March afternoon, fierce cold, yet for Leahy the great outdoors was an appealing prospect. He craved fresh air.

"Give my best to your mammy and daddy now, Michael. Sorry, I mean Garda O'Driscoll. It's been a while since they moved from the parish, but I often think of them, and how proud they were when Kathleen was married." This from the man with the notoriously bad memory. "They must be awful proud of you."

"So they are, Father. I'll be sure to tell them you were asking for them."

"Hate to break this up, but we've got more visits to make." Leahy was keen to move on, to walk and to think. That thinking might include a trip down his own memory lane. Another parish, another priest, another lifetime ago. He would try not to draw comparisons though sometimes that was nigh impossible. Too long in the presence of any of these animals and he could taste that taste again.

"Goodbye, Father. Thank you for your time."

Ahern extended his right hand to shake the Inspector's, who produced at the same moment his card bearing all his contact numbers. It was a ploy he had devised some time before, rather than have to shake the hand of a suspect. He used to wonder if his own hand would ever be clean again, so was happy to avoid contact whenever possible. Ahern's fingers were yellow stained, the nails long, cracked, crusted with dirt. With these he touched the Sacred Host.

"If you can think of anything, I'd be grateful if you'd get in touch. My numbers, my mobile, all on there."

The light in the hall was dimmer than the parlour yet Leahy caught a look in the old man's eyes; it was that unmistakeable flash of intelligence from a cornered wild animal when it thinks it has an escape route.

"Like I said, my memory's not what it was..."

"Anything. Anything at all."

The two police officers returned to their car.

"Well, that was a waste of time. Yer man told us feck all," Michael O'Driscoll moaned as he unlocked the car for the ride back to the station.

"You've got a bit to learn yet, young Michael. He told us plenty, the fucking kiddy fiddler. Let him sweat a day or two, then we'll pay him another visit. Now feck off back to the office, you. I fancy a spot of this wonderful fresh air."

Inside the chilly parlour, John Ahern twitched the grey net curtain back into place. It crackled with age and the lack of laundering. He had watched the Gards go their separate ways and then he went to the kitchen where he poured a large Jameson to toast himself on a successful outcome. He'd seen them off, that Leahy character and O'Driscoll, who'd always been as thick as they come. Probably the only job he could get, with the Gards. Fancy bringing the gingernut along, they probably thought it would throw him. Gobshites.

He tossed away Leahy's card, there'd be no further need for it. They were no match for him, an educated man, a man of the cloth.

Yes, he'd seen the back of them all right. Of that he was convinced.

MY NAME IS MARY SUTHERLAND

My name is Mary Sutherland. I am fifteen, though my Dad says going on fifty.

Tell it in your own words they said. So I will.

I'm sitting in a room with a long narrow window way up high. It's made of those glass brick things that my Dad's wife likes so much. She's got them in their new bathroom because she thinks they look stylish. I think they look like the bottoms of dirty milk bottles. She likes the way they let in light. I prefer the dark and this room suits me just fine, now all that noise and carry-on back at the house has stopped. There's a huge mirror on one wall and I'll bet they're all sitting on the other side watching me. I've seen that sort of thing on the telly. I like Inspector Frost best because he makes me laugh. Dad's wife says I laugh too loud and she can't follow the plot. She sometimes paints her toenails when we're in the lounge and makes the room smell of pear drops.

I'm wearing a white sort of all in one thing, a kind of baby-grow, with a small hood attached and there's elastic round the hood and cuffs. The elastic at the wrists is tight, it makes my hands and wrists look like a baby's, as if there are rubber bands digging into the flesh. If I pull the hood up it puckers round my face, I can feel it pinching. They've taken my glasses away but I bet I'd look really mental if I put them on with this hood thing drawn tight round my cheeks. For my fifteenth birthday Dad was going to pay for some really nice contact lenses, but his wife said we couldn't afford them, so he got me a compilation hits CD instead. It was called 'Sounds of the Summer' and my birthday was in March.

"Bound to be something on there you'll like," he said.

"Yeah, great," I said.

"You must let me have a listen sometime."

It was pants. I only played it the once, I didn't want to hurt his feelings.

Funny just now, I thought I saw one of the rats behind me when I was looking in the mirror, and when I turned round there was nothing there. But like I said, they've taken my glasses. They made me shower and wash my hair too, after they'd picked through it with these big tweezer things and found some bits of bone and other stuff. That took like forever; my hair is long and brown and wiry – Sophie Carter in my year says it's like bum fluff. Hers is long too, but golden and glossy and it moves a lot; she could be in a telly ad. Her best friend, Carly Howell, says I look like a Brillo pad on top of a Christmas pudding – our school uniform's brown, you see. I don't have a best friend.

When my Dad married his wife two years ago I wanted to be bridesmaid. I heard her tell one of her mates on the phone that there'd be a world shortage of pink tulle. She was always on the phone. I was given a basket of rose petals to take to the registry office. I forgot about them though, and left them in the bog and couldn't scatter them on the steps for the photos outside like I was supposed to. Dad gave me one of his 'how can you be so dense?' looks. You can't really see me in the wedding photos much, except in one where I'm just behind the nephew of one of Dad's workmate's wives; you can see the light bouncing off my glasses.

After a few months in our old home we moved to this big place called The Thatched House. We needed the space apparently and besides it was near her family. I had to go to a different school, something to do with a catchment area, but Dad's wife said he'd be saving on fees and they'd need the money for when the new baby came along and for improvements to her new home. Not 'our' new home, just 'hers.'

At first I liked the house; it smelled interesting, sort of dusty, a bit like old people do when you sit next to them on a bus. It probably sounds daft but I thought the house liked me too. Inside there were loads of dark corners and little rooms and nooks and crannies where I could sit for hours just thinking about stuff, about my Mum, and how it had been before she got sick and stuff. It was all right until Dad's wife got this firm of builders in and they started banging around and making some of the little rooms into one big one, like the kitchen. It looks like something out of a magazine now, all granite and maple, and lots of those lights that are flat in the ceiling.

I saw the first of the rats when they were doing up the kitchen. Perhaps a family of them was disturbed with all the racket that was going on. One of the builders chased it with a baseball bat and clubbed it to death, and it took some battering, believe me. Dad's wife couldn't look. She squealed, a bit like the rat, and held her tummy where the baby was. Dad thought we should keep the baseball bat handy just in case there were any more, so he cleaned it up and kept it by the kitchen door, which was new and had double glazed panes in it. Before there'd been some nice old stable doors which didn't quite close properly and used to let the draughts in.

Bit by bit the house began to lose its personality. After the kitchen was finished the builders started work on the main bedroom and bathroom upstairs, and then they had another of the bedrooms made into a kind of nursery so it would be nice when the baby came. She said my bedroom would have to wait, but a lick of paint would probably be all it would need. She gave me their old bedspread to brighten things up a bit, which I didn't mind, because it was the one that Mum and Dad used to sleep under. One day when I'd sneaked into their swanky new bathroom to find some aspirin, I thought I heard a little clack clack clack noise on the floor tiles. I turned really quickly and I swear something big and grey vanished up near the bath panel where the builders had left a gap.

I didn't say anything to anyone. It seemed like the rats were still trying to hold on to what was theirs, and they weren't ready to give up the house just yet. I don't like rats much, but they sort of had a point.

Anyway, after we'd been there for a few months, Dad's wife had the baby, a girl they called Rosie. She was like a little rosebud actually, all small and curled up and pretty, though I could hardly get near her for backslapping and coo-ing relations. Dad's wife and her sisters and all her girlfriends made the baby's room sound like a pigeon loft. Dad seemed like he could explode with happiness when he looked at little Rosie and I wonder if he'd ever looked at me like that.

After a few weeks, things sort of got back to normal. Dad's wife continued treating me like I was something she'd brought in on her shoe, and at school I was a bit of a curiosity for a while, what with being new there and the baby in the house and all that. Mostly I was ignored.

Rosie's first Christmas came and Dad's wife put up decorations but they were all black and silver, bits of bent wire and black baubles; she'd seen some style consultant on the telly do it and she thought it was really cool, so she copied the look, even though we'd brought masses of lovely coloured lights and tinsel and stuff that Mum used to put up in our old home. The house looked really odd; the refurbished bits looked sort of underdressed – except she called it 'minimalist' – and the rest of the house looked plain daft. On Christmas Eve it was very windy and the old windows let in gusts of air, as if the house was sighing. The more Dad's wife was banging on about double glazing, the more the house seemed to sigh. I took some rubbish out that night. I might be big but I'm not noisy, and as I got to the bins I saw a rat gnawing on something, I saw his red eyes, crimson slits out there in the dark, then he saw me. He raised himself up a bit and seemed to smell the air about him Clack clack clack and he was gone.

I didn't tell anybody.

On Christmas Day some of her lot came round, and the kitchen was full of chattering women wearing too much make up, and the smell of the turkey was all mixed in with the smell of their flirty perfumes. Gross. When they weren't in the kitchen they'd swoop on Rosie and cluck and fuss all over her. The men stayed in the lounge with Dad and drank whiskey and barked with laughter at each other's jokes. Of course photos were taken, as it was Rosie's first Christmas. Dad's wife said I could make myself useful and take a few snaps. I suppose they're still in the camera. Dad was about to take a photo of me holding Rosie but then his wife came in with a witches' brew of mulled something or other, and he sort of forgot.

Tell it in your own words, they said, exactly as you remember it.

On New Year's Eve Dad and his wife were going off to

some party. Babysitters are hard to find and very expensive then, or as Dad said 'worth their weight in gold' and she said if that was the case they wouldn't be able to afford me then. She thought that was well funny. Anyway they got me to look after Rosie. Nobody'd invited me to anything, so it would be just me and the baby in the house together. I'd looked after her before and we got on alright. Dad had given me a mobile phone for Christmas, and he said I could spend the evening texting my friends. Yeah, right. I had nobody to text. Just before they left, as a joke, he brought me the baseball bat from the kitchen, to scare off any burglars.

"Or she could just sit on them," said his wife. She left the baby monitor switched on in the lounge so I could hear if Rosie woke up or cried or anything.

It was nice when they went. They hadn't done up the lounge yet, but I'm not supposed to call it 'lounge' because she said that was common. She wanted to put in new windows and take out the panelling and paint over the beams and buy cream leather sofas and display a single lily in a tall glass vase. I liked the room the way it was.

There wasn't anything good on the telly, so I got myself a nice meal of oven chips and pepperoni pizza, and settled down to read a book I'd been given for Christmas about a boy who finds a dead dog on the lawn. I was warm and full and I could hear Rosie over the monitor. She was making those funny little wuffling noises in her sleep.

After a bit, I'm not sure when, I thought I saw a movement out of the corner of my eye; was it something behind the curtain? Probably it was just the draughty old windows having a laugh, before they ended up with all the other rubbish. Don't know. Then a bit later, I thought I heard a clack clack clack noise in the hall; it was a sound I'd heard before but couldn't quite remember where or when.

Old houses make noises though, don't they? They yawn and stretch and scratch themselves like old people, because old people don't care any more what anyone thinks of them, and they often end up on the rubbish too.

I went back to my book. I think I might have dozed a bit. Everything was quiet. The house was quiet. The baby monitor was quiet. I picked it up, held it to my ear. There seemed to be no sound at all. I turned up the volume control to max and then thought I could hear something at last. I listened harder and harder, and the sounds I could make out weren't the usual ones the baby made; these were something else. I listened and concentrated very hard, and it was as if I was listening to the uncles on Christmas Day guzzling and slurping on the turkey drumsticks.

Yes, that was it. I was listening to chewing and gorging.

I don't know what made me do it, but I picked up the baseball bat, and began the journey from the lounge up to Rosie's room. I'd done it loads of times before, now suddenly it seemed a very long way off. I think my mouth was very, very dry, and I think my palms were very, very wet, and I had that funny muzzy sensation too, like when you're at the swimming baths and you go underwater and can hear all the muffled sounds of everyone on the surface.

I went into the hall, slowly, slowly up the stairs, along the landing, towards the baby's room and then after about a thousand years I stood in the doorway and looked in. Everything seemed to be okay: the baa-lambs still larked about on the wallpaper, the moon-face nightlight that looked like a Chinaman gave off a nearly-yellow glow, and the mobile of bunny rabbits bounced over her cot.

It had all gone quiet. The central heating had gone to sleep. The windows had stopped rattling. The house was holding its breath, like it was waiting for something.

And then there was a tearing, a ripping sort of sound, not of cloth but of something else, and a movement from the cot. There was another noise, somewhere between a cry and a gasp and I thought Rosie was waking up and might need a cuddle, so I went straight into the room towards her, and there, sitting on her little face and pulling at a bit of her shoulder was a rat, big and fat and grey and sleek and hard, and it turned, honest it did, it turned its head to look at me with those eyes, those blood red slits that passed for eyes, and I could see its teeth too and they were grey and red it had bits of Dad's wife's baby in its teeth and so I lifted up that baseball bat and I brought it down on the cot with every single bit of strength I had in me and there was a squeal or was it a shriek and a flurry of movement and so I did it again and again and again until there was nothing left nothing left at all and then I can't really remember too much after that apart from feeling sick and sticky and out of breath like I'd been running for the bus and my glasses steamed up so I couldn't see anything then the next thing I know there's voices and screaming and howling like it's Halloween but it can't be Halloween because it's New Year's Eve right and I saw Dad and I saw his wife and I didn't remember her wearing a red dress I thought it was cream yeah that's right she'd gone out in a cream dress and she had on long red gloves too red right up to her elbows and she was holding this floppy rag doll thing to her and making this noise and then there were more voices new voices strange voices and bodies and lights outside blue and flashing and someone took me outside and it had started to rain and my hands were tied behind me and I think I was pushed and pulled a bit and someone banged my head against a white car door and I said, "I killed it. I killed the rat."

My name is Mary Sutherland. I am fifteen.

THE EFFICIENT USE OF REASON

The Code of Canon Law states: "Merely ecclesiastical laws bind those who have been baptized in the Catholic Church or received into it, possess the efficient use of reason, and, unless the law expressly provides otherwise, have completed seven years of age." (Codex Iuris Canonici 11).

Belén and Jimena had a friendship made in heaven. One was born to lead, firm yet tender, while the other was a willing acolyte, submissive though far from repressed. Despite this seeming unbalance they shared everything, from hair ribbons to skipping ropes, from kittens to Playmobil sets. If one was happy, the other rejoiced; if one was sad, the other grieved. They laughed and breathed almost as one. Sometimes when both dark heads were bent over their crayons or a fluffy object, it could take any one of their parents more than a heartbeat to pick out his/her daughter. They met at nursery school and had been friends for more than three years, nearly half their respective life times, and now attended the same primary school. Life was sunny and funny and they couldn't imagine the day when they would not be each other's closest confidante.

It couldn't last.

One spring morning shortly after Easter and the Holy Week processions, Belén went to school as usual but her friend was not there. She had planned to show her a drawing of the Virgin Mary that she had done from memory: it showed the vast statue borne aloft on a float decked with enormous silver urns filled with roses of the palest pink. It will come as no surprise that the girls loved pink; it was their colour of choice. Jimena had liked the white flowers too, but decided that pink were nicer once Belén had declared them her favourites. They loved the Virgin Mary; her statues were to be seen all over town during the Holy Week processions, and though she looked sad and wept tears of pearl on some of the effigies, the girls thought she was a real beauty. They found her irresistible with her alabaster skin and eyes raised heavenwards, dressed in lace and black velvet; sometimes she was cloaked in blue, swooning in the arms of John the Baptist at the foot of the Cross as she witnessed the death of her only Son. Ai-eee!

So discovering that her little amiga was not waiting for her before they were summoned for morning classes, Belén was a tad nonplussed. She hoped Jimena wasn't ill, but their mothers had not spoken as they did when either child was out of sorts. Hopefully she would find out when lessons finished at 2 o'clock and Mamá came to walk her home. The only thing the girls didn't do together was walk to and from school, unless one was going to the other's to play. Their homes were equidistant from the school, although in opposite directions, and the four parents deemed any detours completely unnecessary. Sure enough, just after 2 o'clock, Belén saw her mother talking to two others at the school gates; there was much shaking of heads and downcast eyes, rather like the Mater Dolorosa herself. Still wearing her school smock and carrying her little pink backpack decorated with darker pink flowers, she hurtled towards Mamá. Completely ignoring the other grown ups, she blurted out the news about her friend's no-show.

"Mamá, guess what? Jimena didn't come today! Can we go to her house? Maybe she's sick? Can we go there now, Mamá? Oh, say we can? Can we? Mamá?"

"Belén, manners! Now say hello to Señora Martín, and Señora Torres."

"Hola, Señoras," Belén dimpled and bobbed at the

ladies, who were waiting for their sons, in whom the child had no interest at all. They both bent to kiss the little girl and then all three señoras resumed the mask of tragedy.

"Very sad news today, chica. Señora Torres says that Jimena's granny died last night so all the family have gone down to Cádiz."

Unlike Belén's family, where her sole surviving grandparent lived with them, Jimena's were dotted around Andalucia: the recently deceased grandmother in Cádiz, her surviving but amicably divorced spouse in Seville, while the grandfather on the distaff side lived in Málaga.

"Oh, poor Jimena. She has no more grandmas. She can share mine! Abuelita is fat enough for two of us!"

At which point Señora Diaz decided it was time to take her daughter home to where her fat granny and baby brother waited.

Some days passed and Belén mooched and meandered without her best friend's company. The curse of having a very, very best friend is that when said boon companion is away, it is harder to fit in with others, but Belén muscled her way into a few skipping games and colouring sessions, so not all was lost.

Soon normal service was resumed. Bélen entered the school grounds one morning to see a small crowd congregating around a familiar head, the shiny chestnut locks of her beloved pal.

"Jimena! It's lovely to see you." Belén ran to embrace her friend, pushing her way through the group. Jimena returned the hug, but kept a newspaper at arm's length to prevent it being crushed.

"I missed you, Bel, but now I'm back."

"Sorry about your grandma, but you can always have a share of mine. She's fat and there's plenty to go round, but Mamá said I mustn't say that."

At this Jimena giggled. Another girl, Maite, known for her fierce animal impressions, lunged for the paper in Jimena's hand.

"Show me, show me again, or I'll roar like a tiger!" she demanded. She was scary.

"What have you got there? What's so important?" asked Belén. Jimena was *her* friend after all, and therefore she had priority.

"It's the notice in the paper about Granny. Look, see here, it mentions Grandpa, and then there's Papa and Uncle Manolo and Uncle Francisco, well of course he's dead and I never knew him so he doesn't count. Anyway he gets a cross by his name you see, so you know he's dead, and next there's my mum, Marta, and Aunt Susanna, but look look look, here's me, my name: Jimena! I've got my name in the paper. Jimena! Jimena!"

Their teacher summoned them for the beginning of lessons. This curtailed the excitement of the newly famous Jimena and her friends, but she promised to show the paper privately to her special friend later.

And so she did. They had a mid morning break and the girls scuttled away to their favourite corner in the school grounds, under the shade of a massive olive tree. Jimena produced the paper from her backpack, which was pink like Belén's, but unlike hers, was decorated with pictures of My Little Pony instead of dark pink flowers. Belén thought My Little Pony was rather babyish but refrained from saying so out of kindness. Jimena pressed at the creases in the newspaper with her fingers, careful not to get any marks on it from the morning's artwork.

"See, here it is, my name in the paper. I'm famous! Of course it took Granny to die and that makes it bad, but it's really really good too. Don't you think?"

Belén studied the text, slowly absorbing all the information:

"Josefa Pons Ruiz died on April 12, aged 82 years.

Rest in peace.

Her husband Adolfo Garcia Gomez; sons Jaime, Manolo, Francisco†; daughters-in-law Marta, Susanna; grandchildren Jimena, Pedro, Cristina, Alvaro, Josefa; brothers Diego, Francisco; all nephews, nieces, sisters-in-law, cousins and friends are respectfully requested to attend the requiem Mass to celebrate her life on April 15 at the Iglesia de San Felipe Neri.

She will always be in our hearts."

The girls bent over the piece of paper and Jimena read aloud once more, in case Belén hadn't quite grasped it. When she got to her own name she said, "My name goes first because I'm the eldest child of Granny's eldest. See? *Jimena*, that's me, then *Pedro*. Then it's Uncle Manolo's children, my cousins, but Uncle Francisco didn't have any, he died young."

"Why?" asked Belén.

"Mamá said he had Aids."

"What's that?"

"Don't know, but he was very thin. Granny showed me a photo."

At which point, Maite and her two friends Ana and Sofia came sidling up. They were not present for the first reading before school.

"Jimena, Sofia doesn't believe you've got your name in the paper, she says you're making it up," said Maite, cutting to the chase.

"Am not," said Jimena, jutting out a defiant chin.

"Show me," demanded Sofia. Ana hovered nearby, inspecting the contents of her nose that now glistened on her finger's end.

Jimena took the paper from Belén, proudly parading her name once more for all to see.

"Wow!" said Sofia. Ana wiped her finger on her smock and leaned in.

"Weeeee!"

Maite squealed like a pig in reply, and the noises brought over more of the schoolmates, even some of the boys came for a quick look.

"You're famous, Jimena," said Roderigo. "Look everyone, Jimena's really famous, like Iker Casillas, or the king or... or... or..."

"Rafa?" suggested Diego. His sister played tennis and was into the Mallorcan superstar big time.

"Yay!" said Jimena, getting quite carried along with it all.

"Jimena's in the paper, Jimena's really famous..." someone chanted, and then someone else joined in, then one or two others.

"Jimena's in the paper, Jimena's really famous..." they all chorused.

Apart from Belén.

At supper with her family that night, Belén looked across the table at her chubby, cheerful Grandmother, her Abuelita, as she was known. She watched her eat, and bustle round, and help to feed three-year old Pedro when he missed his mouth. He liked to make farmyard noises while he ate and smaller items of his meal would travel some distance. Belén thought about Jimena and the paper and how everyone had said she was famous. Jimena was delighted with the attention, though Belén was not so sure. What if Maite and the others started trying to claim her for themselves? What if they wanted to play with her and invite her to play at their houses without Belén? They always did everything together and for Jimena to reach the dizzy heights of stardom without her was inconceivable. Unbearable. Intolerable.

Something must be done.

A solution presented itself easier that she dreamed possible. Little Pedro loved his farmyard set best of all his toys; it consisted of a green plastic tractor in which sat a jolly red-faced farmer and attached to the rear was a trailer containing one pig, one cow and one chicken. He liked to play with it on the upper hallway at the top of the stairs. The stairs were steep. It was an old townhouse refurbished and remodelled by their parents but several original features remained: the staircase, the shutters, the oak floorboards. The staircase was never a problem before Luisa and Enrique had children and before her mother came to live with them, an overweight lady who was often out of breath. Everyone had to be constantly on their guard. Pedro, being only three, hadn't paid much attention when Mamá warned him about leaving his toys near the top of the stairs in case somebody tripped and fell one day, so it was down to Belén, as the responsible older sibling, to keep an eye on his playthings. Mamá couldn't always be in attendance.

Belén thought long and hard and was very quiet that evening. Her parents wondered if she was sickening for something, and Abuelita placed a hand on her unfevered brow before pronouncing her "healthier than a pear." She was a nice Granny, the only one she had, and didn't want to cause her any harm or pain. However, because she was the last surviving grandparent, she was also Belén's only chance.

The following morning Mamá left to go shopping with Pedro in tow; Papá was working and Abuelita was late rising, as she so often was. She took her time in the mornings, preferring to linger and make sure she was entirely ready to face the world, rather than trundle up and down that infernal staircase. She thought Luisa and her husband were stark raving mad doing up an old house and she so envied her friend, Doña Carlotta, who lived in a nice modern apartment with her son and his friend. There was an elevator and a terrace and the Doña had her own bathroom and didn't have to share with two children, adorable though they sometimes were.

She pinned up her hair, as she had done for the past fifty-four years or so, almost without thought. She knew the family laughed at her bedtime pigtail but it saved much carry on in the mornings, when there was a husband and children to be cared for... ah no, that was *then*. A long time ago, when the hair was still dark chestnut brown, just like Belén's. Old habits die hard. Ai-eee! Her favourite dress was laid out on the bed, a wrap-over creation in shades of brown and coral flowers. Not for her the widow's black! She was due to meet her friends for chocolate and churros at La Vega once Luisa was back with Pedrito. Plenty of time to prepare. And Señor Ortega might be passing, one never knew. A little more rouge perhaps? Or maybe a touch less? She didn't want to look like a clown. Certainly some eyeshadow, blue or turquoise, just a touch to bring out the colour of her eyes. Applying it would be easier if only the hands didn't shake so much.

Then from downstairs a crash, a clatter, then a scream, a shriek, a screech of what? Pain? Fear? Belén! Whatever was happening?

While the old lady dithered and paused, another heartrending yelp cleaved the air. It sounded like a whipped puppy.

"Abuelita! Please! Please come quick! I need you," howled her granddaughter.

This was serious. No time to get her glasses, or put on shoes, she drew her robe about her, no time to tie it tidily, and left her room.

From downstairs she heard a whimpering, sobbing Belén.

"It's all right, little one, Abuelita's coming, I'm com..."

In her haste to reach the distraught child, her daughter's first born, she didn't notice Pedro's toys at the top of the stairs and she didn't notice the trailing sash of her bathrobe.

Sash. Toys. Barefoot.

The sash wrapped about her ankle, snagged on the toy and her foot caught in the plastic trailer that was filled with the farmyard animals and was drawn by the green tractor. Her foot twisted, her ankle snapped and she stumbled headfirst down the staircase, her foot still bizarrely wedged in the toy trailer, like an ill-fitting shoe.

In the kitchen Belén helped herself to a biscuit. She listened to the thump, crump and the cut off cry for the Mother of God to assist her, as her Grandmother travelled down the stairs in an unwontedly short time. There was no muttering, no shuffling, no hanging on to the banister, no tiptoeing gingerly in her unsuitable shoes; just a thump, whump, shout, shriek, slap, accompanied by the oink of the farmyard pig and the moo of the farmyard cow and the cluck of the farmyard chicken as they slammed and banged downstairs with her. As she landed at the foot of the stairs the old lady's neck snapped as easily as her ankle had at the beginning of her rapid descent.

Belén finished her biscuit, listening for signs of life from the hallway.

Silence.

Perfecto!

She righted the kitchen chair and replaced in the cupboards the pans that she had dropped on the tiled floor. Then she rubbed and rubbed and rubbed her eyes until they were red and sore.

And waited.

Much later that day when the police had left, satisfied that it was nothing other than a small domestic tragedy, and Abuelita's chubby broken body had been removed to the funeral home, Belén cuddled up to her mother who sat drained and limp.

"Mamá, when will my name be in the paper...?"

HOW I GOT HERE

There was something about her. She reminded me of someone from back when. Taller, heavier, though there was something around the eyes.

She picked me up one afternoon in a coffee shop in Lower Marsh. I'd seen her around. I've got the time now to think it through from that first meeting, though there's probably not much left. Time, I mean. I feel remarkably calm, despite this shit state of affairs. Got some feeling again in my feet, my legs, but can't kick my way out of here, there isn't the room. I may as well just wait it out.

We went to bars and restaurants, plays at the National, and walked along the river to my place, handy for her to get to work at St Thomas's if she was on earlies. She didn't move in her toothbrush or a change of underwear, didn't try to insinuate herself and I liked that. Women often leave something behind, so they'll have an excuse to come back for it. And it's usually the ones you don't ask again anyway. I've lived in my flat for seven years, kept my life simple, never wanted the clutter of another body round the place, and certainly not some silly tart's yoga mat or bottle of moisturiser. I don't want anyone marking my territory.

Another thing I liked was that she didn't talk about herself all the time, or her 'feelings.' She let me ramble on about work and she listened when I started on my pet rants. I asked her, why do women always want to change a man? I mean, I said, you go out with a guy because you like the look of him, right? So why the little hints about his shirts or the length of his hair or whatever?

It was a bit of a favourite, a theme I warmed to after a couple. I'm right though, aren't I? All too soon it starts. You pass a shop and hear: You'd look so-o-o cool in that jacket. Or, I saw some fabulous boots in Great Compton Street, – it was always places like that, never Dalston or Croydon, – they'd be great on you. Oh, here we fucking go, I'd think. I stopped telling them my birthday.

Anyway, she, Sophie, didn't come out with any of that. Everything was fine. Once I left her asleep in bed, and when I got back after work she hadn't moved anything, or fluffed up cushions or whatever it is girls like to do. She just got dressed and left. No long hairs in the shower; no tender notes; nothing.

So, one night she asked me over to hers for a change. She was off to the States for a month. None of that 'will you miss me?' crap. Said she'd cook Thai. Great, I said. It would be like a farewell dinner, she said. So what time d'you want me round, I said. Seven, eight, whenever, she said. Didn't tie me down, that was good.

I got round to hers after eight. No flatmates; no cats. I had some wine; she wasn't drinking, was prepping the food. I watched her. She moved the butcher's knife like a pro through peppers and chicken. Her hands didn't look too clean though, dirty nails. Funny that, her being a nurse.

I sat, waiting for this meal. She chopped, but no sign of actual cooking yet, you understand. Had another glass of wine, then another, told her about my day surrounded by the fuckwits at work, the usual.

I'd not had any lunch. Had a few beers after work and the wine was getting to me, a heavy old chardonnay, bit acidic, and I wondered if I was ever going to get fed.

Hungry? she asked.

Ravenous, I said. Haven't eaten since this morning.

Won't be long now, she said.

She came and sat beside me; she was holding something, hiding something. A hand on my thigh. I thought she was rubbing it, but I felt a scratch then a stinging. Then a... not sure what exactly.

Nearly ready, she said.

I needed the bathroom. Put my glass on the table.

Fingers were numb and I knocked over a photo. It was of her and an older couple, her parents probably, and another girl. Like her only paler, thinner. Little round glasses.

Gotta pee, I said.

She replaced the photo. I tried to stand, legs seemed unwilling to comply. Fucksake, I'd only had three or four glasses of wine. Coupla beers. Must be losing it.

Mind that, she said. The photo back in place. I looked at it. Didn't really see it though, if you know what I mean.

Family?

Yeah.

Mum, dad? I asked, still trying to stand while observing the pleasantries.

Yeah, and my baby sister.

Nice. Don't suppose you could give me a hand up, I said, big, strong girl like you? Don't want to piss all over your nice sofa. I slurred: 'pish' and 'nishe shofa.'

It's had worse on it, she said. My sister's blood when she killed herself, for instance.

Then she talked. Lots. She told me about her sister, frail, pale Alice, who fell in love, got dumped, never recovered.

Alice.

Shit. I'd known an Alice. Skinny little thing.

I remembered.

Alice came back from Camden Market with some cushions for my place, at which point I knew it was over. Told her on the spot. Didn't take it too well.

Long story short, breathing is a bit of a problem just now.

She put down a syringe, guess that's what had scratched me, stood me up, half dragged, half carried me outside to the back garden. My mouth had stopped working, everything had except my bladder and I pissed myself. Didn't feel it, saw it. Dark spreading round my crotch.

There was a hole dug deep, and in it there was a man sized wooden box; well, a coffin actually. She dropped me into it. I didn't hurt myself. Didn't shout. Couldn't.

She stood over me. You remember Alice, don't you? she said. You can't begin to understand what she felt, you're not capable. You can share something with her instead. She's been lying in the cold, hard ground for two years. Now let's see how you like it.

She placed the lid on top. She hammered in nails. There was music playing somewhere. She started to shovel earth onto the box. Clump, dump, it went. Clump, dump. It was rhythmic, almost sent me to sleep.

Then it went quiet. Very quiet.

Yeah. She said she was going to the States for a month.

HIS FAMILY

You know the moment when a police officer settles the prisoner in the car? You must have seen it countless times in television dramas. Hand on the prisoner's head to protect it always. It's a simple enough task and yet sometimes one of the hardest parts of my job. On more than one occasion I have wanted to smash the prisoner's skull against the doorframe, when I have just witnessed his, or sometimes even her, handiwork. Reminds me of the old police brutality joke. Question: How did the copper crack open his egg? Answer: He didn't, sarge, it slipped on its way down to the cell. What would push an upstanding professional officer, highly trained to deal with any eventuality, to seriously consider it?

Damien Roth was singularly unremarkable in appearance, a fact alone that could have made him special. His lightly pocked skin had the slightly oily texture of damp putty; his hair, to describe it as sandy over dignified it, his eyelashes were practically nonexistent, the colour of his eyes somewhere between dun and khaki; he was small, almost dainty, yet wiry and strong. There was something of the jockey about him. Very self contained, strangely he had no presence, no aura, and his mushroom coloured hospital uniform did little to dispel the sensation. He was easy to overlook.

He said it was simple enough to gain employment at the hospital two years ago. Checks were less stringent then and there was always a demand for porters, those unsung and unheralded operatives who ferry around the sick, the dying and the dead, or even just some of their component parts. Wheelchairs and stretchers for the whole or nearly whole;

buckets for the discarded limbs. All in a day's work. Very nasty, but someone's got to do it.

Damien enjoyed patrolling the hospital grounds and corridors even when not on duty. Had he been questioned about this, he would have responded that it was important to find the fastest and easiest routes round the hospital's sprawl for his charges, such was his diligence. He was unremarkable and quiet, did not join the union to picket for better pay and conditions, but would always contribute whenever asked for a donation to a colleague's gift. He appeared punctually for his shifts and never watched the clock when going home time was approaching. According to his superiors, all in all a model employee.

The hospital consisted of two buildings on the same site. The newer part, built at the end of the twentieth century, accommodated Accident and Emergency, wards and operating theatres; the older building, four storeys high and constructed in the middle of the preceding century, housed only the administration functions for personnel and finance, in a small suite of rooms confined to the ground floor. When bureaucracy and fundraising permitted, they too intended to move to another new extension. The first and second floors were used for storage, though who would want elderly rusting bedsteads, trolleys and wheelchairs, bent food trays and chipped utility crockery? The top two floors were surplus to requirements, and nobody we spoke to among the hospital staff could ever recall the need to visit them. There had been a grandiose scheme to redevelop this older wing into luxury flats, but in the light of recent events such homes may prove undesirable.

Damien Roth's knowledge of the hospital layout naturally included the older part. Of particular interest was the very top floor, served at the rear entrance by an elderly if functional lift, which was accessed by a concertina door. It grated and clattered but reached its destination for all that, like some decrepit old dowager wheezing her way upstairs to the attic.

The windows on the top floors hadn't been cleaned for literally decades. Light barely filtered through even on the brightest of days, while cracked linoleum on the floors rendered the surfaces unsafe in the half-light. Damien Roth, however, was as sure of his footing as he was of everything else. Over a period of time he had been gathering very basic items of furniture: a bed, some chairs, a table, some filing cabinets. He found too a defunct television set, which he placed on top of a filing cabinet, as he gradually assembled his twilight home. Cups and plates, moth eaten blankets, old stained pillows. All the domestic paraphernalia needed was found two floors down, and transported aloft.

But there was something missing.

William Mason sat in the hospital reception area with his overnight bag on his lap, waiting for his daughter Dorothy, to come and collect him. She was rather late, but she had such a busy and full life, and she said she'd pick him up after she had dropped her husband off at the airport, away on another business trip. He was due to stay at Dorothy's only while her husband was overseas for a short period of convalescence after a nasty bout of emphysema, before returning to his own ground floor flat. This was near enough to his daughter for emergencies, but not too close so it interfered with her interesting and varied schedule.

William checked his wristwatch. She really was very late. No doubt the traffic was bad, and it was asking a lot of her to come and collect him. She'd be along soon enough, and then they'd get to her house and have a lovely cup of tea, and he would wait for his grandsons to come in from school and…

"Hallo, Mr Mason, you've been here a while, haven't you?"

It was that nice porter, the quiet fellow. Darren, or something.

"Darren, hello. I'm waiting for my daughter, she's coming to collect me. I expect she'll be along any time now..."

"Yes, I know, I've just seen her. She's having a spot of bother finding a place to park, so she's asked me to take you out to her."

"Thank you Darren, thank you very much, if it's no trouble."

"No trouble at all, Mr Mason. You don't want to sit here all day, it's like a mad house. Let's get you outside."

Damien released the brake on William's wheelchair, and steered him through the controlled bedlam of hospital reception. He pushed him around the side of the building, away from its clamour and security, towards the old wing. William was confused; his lungs and his legs were all but useless, but there was little wrong with his eyesight.

"Where are we going, Darren?"

"She said she'd wait around the back here, so you just relax and enjoy the ride. We can take a short cut through the old building."

William Mason relaxed and enjoyed the ride as he'd been instructed, thinking that the longed for cup of tea was getting nearer.

"If you don't mind me asking, Mr Mason, how old are you?"

"All the sixes, clickety click," replied his passenger, a lifelong fan of bingo. Dorothy and her husband preferred bridge and backgammon.

"Perfect," said Damien, "that's about the same age as my dad."

They entered the old wing by the back entrance, and in the far distance the sounds of office life trickled down the corridors. The lift was already on the ground floor, the door open like a yawning mouth at feeding time. Its mechanism could not be heard in the administration suites. Damien had checked. William, curious if not concerned, tried to turn round in the wheelchair and question Damien, but the porter just gave him an encouraging pat on the shoulder and shushed him, as if a child. They rode up in it to the top floor where the air hung heavy and musty, as if undisturbed for decades. Damien pushed him down a maze of corridors and eventually they arrived at a large open area with chairs and a television set. William was having some difficulty getting his breath in the stale atmosphere, added to a growing sense of unease. Ignoring his questions, Damien lifted him out of the wheelchair, sat him in one of the upright armchairs, and leant over him to adjust his scarf. A casual observer might have been touched by his seeming concern for the older man.

"Now then, we don't want you catching cold, do we, Mr Mason?"

He gave the scarf a sudden final adjustment, and William fought for breath, his hands flapping aimlessly like injured birds in the vicinity of his throat. His eyes pleaded with Damien's, but all he saw was dun pools, dead and inert. He tried to speak and the last word he would ever utter was a stranger's name:

"Darr-en…"

His eyes bulged while his skin was turning the colour of the blue stripe in his scarf, his protruding tongue a shade somewhere between dove grey and magenta.

"It's *Damien*, Mr Mason. That is, *Damien*."

Eventually Damien Roth loosened the scarf, made sure that William was settled comfortably in his chair, and then made the return journey to the main hospital, and always the considerate employee, replaced the wheelchair in reception. On his way he passed William's daughter. A harassed receptionist, who was still waiting to be relieved for her lunch break at ten minutes to three, had told her that her father had made other arrangements for transport to his own home, owing to the lateness of her arrival. Dorothy was not best pleased with this information, typical of the old bugger, and she resolved to let him stew awhile and not phone him for a day or two.

Audrey Lomax was waiting for her hip replacement operation. Though relatively young, only sixty, she had been plagued for some years with a bad hip, exacerbated by osteoporosis. A major flu epidemic suddenly hit the hospital, staff members from all departments were absenting themselves, and extra cover was needed whenever and wherever possible. Damien, untroubled by the virus, was happy to work extra shifts. He was feeling lucky. Rosters and administration suffered during the flu spell, but Audrey Lomax's hip replacement operation was not affected. Her pre-med was administered, leaving her conscious but light-headed, and Damien was asked to wheel her stretcher to Theatre Number Two, where her surgeon, Mr Reynolds would be awaiting her. On her ward, a telephone rang unanswered for some while. Such luck that Damien happened to be passing and in the absence of any nursing staff, he took the call. He was informed that Mr Reynolds' list was to be cancelled, as he too that very morning had succumbed to the virus. Such luck indeed.

Damien wheeled Audrey Lomax from her ward, from the sanctuary of the new wing to his eyrie in the old building. She was groggy, not fully awake, but when he steered the stretcher from the elderly elevator towards her destination, the smell that greeted her made her gag. William Mason had been sitting in his chair for three days, and he had urinated as he died. Despite her semi-drugged state and the pervading penumbra, Audrey knew there was something very wrong. This wasn't the way to the operating theatre surely? What was this place of foul smelling shadows? She was attempting to breathe through her mouth because of the stench, which she could not easily identify, but she had to try and talk to the porter in whose care she lay. However, like a fly in the spider's web she wasn't so much in his care, as at his mercy. Her voice seemed to belong to somebody else, still she managed:

"What's this place? Where are we?"

Damien paused briefly, produced a small jar of Vick's from his pocket and smeared some under his nose. He ignored her question, the spasm of retching that it produced, and continued wheeling her towards a group of chairs. One of them seemed to be already occupied as far as Audrey could tell, though streaming eyes impaired her vision. The unnameable odour was becoming even stronger.

"Look who I found outside, Dad," he said. "Look who's been hiding from us. Now come on, Mum, let's get you settled and then we can have a nice cup of tea together."

He raised her to a sitting position, lifted her off the trolley and placed her in an upright chair, next to William Mason. He lifted one of William's hands, disregarded the cracking sound he heard as he manoeuvred the wrist, and placed the arid and scaly paw on Audrey's arm, as if in welcome.

"Ah. Look at that, Dad's really pleased to see you," said Damien.

Her sedation was insufficient to lessen the horror of the smell, the sight, and now the touch of the old man, and she tried to scream. A feeble bubbling sound emerged, for her throat had the consistency of sandpaper. She pressed back into the chair, a pathetic attempt to put some little distance between herself and William's mouldering cadaver.

"What's that, Mum, you feeling a bit chilly?" Damien did a comedy mock shiver. "You know, you're right, it is a bit parky in here. Lucky I've got just the thing to warm you up."

He untied the blue striped scarf from William's neck

without disturbing the older man unduly, stood behind Audrey Lomax and tied it round her neck, until she could feel the cold no longer.

Yes, eventually of course the police were summoned. Two patients had seemingly vanished into thin air, no records of removal, no apparent sightings, a hospital in chaos and confusion, and yes of course some of my colleagues searched some of the buildings and the grounds, as it was a very serious matter, but no clues to the whereabouts of William Mason and Audrey Lomax were established. The police station had not escaped the flu epidemic, and we too were under resourced, so our searches were not as thorough as you might reasonably hope for.

Ian Marshall was one of the least badly injured victims of a major traffic accident, which occurred about a week after the police had provided no satisfactory reasons for the disappearance of two not very elderly patients. He sat in Accident and Emergency, stunned and concussed, holding a temporary dressing to a head wound, while waiting for a doctor to check him over thoroughly.

Damien had been quietly ferrying patients from triage to other cubicles or x-ray, doing whatever was required of him. He noticed Ian Marshall sitting unattended and thought perhaps he could help. As he assisted him into a wheelchair he said:

"Has anyone taken your details down yet?"

Ian shook his head, no. He'd given his name to somebody, a very young nurse a while ago, and that was all. Damien was sympathetic.

"That won't do at all, will it? We must get you seen to, mustn't we?"

Ian was really in quite a bad way, and leant back in the

chair as Damien set off. Soon they reached the rear entrance to the old wing, but Ian's eyes were closed. He didn't know where he was, and he cared even less. The car he had been travelling in, the woman who had been beside him, the children fighting on the back seat, the jack-knifed lorry, the damp and greasy road surface; he was reliving the crash in storyboard format.

They seemed to be going up in a lift. The porter spoke to him:

"How old are you?"

He didn't answer, his scrambled thoughts were elsewhere.

The porter punched his shoulder. The question again.

"I said, how old are you?"

"Twenty eight."

"That's nearly perfect," said Damien Roth. "I'm thirty two."

When the elevator arrived at the fourth floor, Damien opened the concertina doors and pushed his newest charge towards the seating area where William and Audrey were waiting for them. Despite Ian's semi comatose state, the odour that assailed his sinus's had the effect of smelling salts on his system. He jerked upright in his wheelchair, and blood flowed down his brow and into his eyes. The scene he beheld spectacularly surpassed the horror of the carnage in which he'd just participated.

It was hell's anteroom. He saw two bloated forms, barely recognisable as a man and a woman, propped upright in high backed chairs. He saw white-grey skin stretched and tinted to a pale merlot with lividity where the blood had pooled post mortem. He smelled gases that escaped from the forms, yielding odours that were at once sweet and sour, foul and foetid. His own blood, fresh and berry red, ran into his mouth, yet he made no attempt to move away or to cry out, for he was utterly transfixed, like a pinned prize butterfly newly added to the collection.

Damien Roth had been moving around somewhere behind him. The only sound was his rubber-soled shoes on the battered lino.

"You shouldn't worry Mum and Dad like that. Staying out late. Say you're sorry."

Damien pinched him, and then punched him harder than before. Ian Marshall licked at the blood on his lips, on his teeth, and tasted copper. He tried to focus on an ancient television set rather than dwell on what sat beside him.

"Oh no, young fellow my lad, no television for you, not until you've said sorry."

Damien pinched him again and again. "Go on, say it. Say sorry."

"Sorry," he whispered.

"Louder," demanded Damien.

"Sorry," he tried again.

"Now say it like you mean it!"

"I'm sorry!"

"There, that's better. Now you can watch telly for as long as you like, can't he, Mum, Dad?"

Ian Marshall felt the warmth of wool against his neck. Damien was wrapping a scarf around him. The scarf smelled of death.

Damien Roth stood back and admired his handiwork: mother, father, younger brother, all united in front of the television set, just like a real family should be. There was only one thing missing to complete the tableau, and he'd kept it by since he'd found it in the gutter, for he knew it would set things off a treat. From a cardboard box he retrieved the body of a cat, two-day-old road kill. It was partially disembowelled and floppy, but he arranged it tenderly on Audrey Lomax's lap as if it were a prize Persian, and set her dried and flaking hand upon it, stroking her cherished pet.

He sat in the remaining chair, enjoying the company once again of his family. This is how it should be: no fighting, no shouting, no father standing at the foot of your bed waiting to say goodnight in his own special way, no mother spending your Christmas money on making her arm look like a pin cushion, no younger brother who liked to play with matches. Perfect.

And so it was we came across them, this family from beyond hell. I had no gloves. I had to touch him, to lead him away from the scene and steer him into the patrol car, my hand protecting his head. He smelled of Vick's. We had been summoned to do another more exhaustive search, and my partner and I had been instructed to check the upper floors of the old wing, even though we'd been reliably informed that we would find absolutely nothing except a few rusting pieces of hospital equipment.

But what we found instead was Damien, his father, his mother, his younger brother, and the family pet, all sitting before the television set, with Damien himself, wearing a blue striped scarf with his porter's uniform, pouring imaginary tea from a chipped tea pot for them all.

Unfortunately during the arrest his skull did make contact with the car's doorframe. Damien Roth is awaiting the results of a claim under the Criminal Injuries Compensation Authority 2008, while I remain suspended on full pay pending an investigation.

THE SANDS ARE MAGIC

After over thirty years the locals are used to her though the newcomers have questions.

"Where does she stay?"

"Isn't anyone with her?"

"She gives me the creeps. Can't they get her to move on?"

She comes for the same two weeks each year, speaks only in shops and cafés to state her needs, and returns always to the same spot on the beach where she sits and waits. And waits.

It was 1977, and the Queen's Silver Jubilee, a good time to be away from west London, from the flat in Goldborne Road.

"Why all the fuss?" Rob had asked. "We pay her enough. All she has to do is ride round in a big car, wave a bit and shake a few hands."

Sitting in the pub on a warm summer's evening, Carl and Annie, and the strange boy with the wispy beard had all agreed with him. So had Susan. "Yes," she said, "it's a fuss."

Rob had served with her husband in Northern Ireland, and was only yards away from him when a sniper in the Falls Road took him out. A single shot to the head. He and Bri had been friends, and he took it hard. Two years later and having left the army, Rob decided to look out his old pal's wife. He'd kept in touch during that time, and so it was no great surprise to her when he turned up armed with a duffle bag, a ghetto blaster, a notebook full of unpublished poetry, and not much else. He had hitched to London from Exeter after his discharge, about which he

112

said little, and asked if he could sleep on the floor at Flat 12A Goldborne Road, until he got himself sorted. He tickled Lucy, then aged six, who protested that she was too big for such nonsense but loved it really; he tossed four year old Nick into the air, and pretended he was about to drop him, then at the crucial moment nestled the boy in strong, tattooed arms. That had been six months ago, in January. He was still at Number 12A, helping out, fixing things, and just before Easter had migrated from the futon in the living room to Susan's bedroom. She liked his attention. It was the first time since Bri that she'd let a man see her naked, touch her, enjoy her, and she reminded herself that she was still a young woman with needs, and not just the mother of Corporal Brian Maynard's fatherless children. All the same Lucy and Nicholas had kept her sane in the dark days after his death, days when she had to deal with his mother's loss besides her own.

"You don't know what I'm going through," the older woman wailed. "Nobody should have to bury their child."

After the session in the pub, Rob put his suggestion to Susan when they were in bed. It was a sticky night in London W10 with hardly a breath of air. The windows were open and also the French doors that lead out to the back. Her landlord, the local council, referred to it as a patio, though really it was only a collection of paving slabs. There was enough space to hang out the washing, and a wall against which Nick practised his football skills. She had tried to grow geraniums in a few pots, but the neighbourhood cats put paid to them. Lucy and her brother would soon be too big to share a room, and Susan had requested a move to larger premises, without revealing anything about her non-paying guest. The DHSS might want to ask questions.

Rob said, "You asleep?"

"Too hot."

"Y'know what we were saying before, all that fuss going

on in London?"

"Yeah?"

"You fancy getting away, getting out of town for a bit?"

Susan shifted to look at him. "What've you got in mind?"

"Cornwall. A holiday. Us four." He moved damp hair away from her brow.

"Lovely idea. What do we use for money?"

"Leave it to your Uncle Rob. We can borrow a mate's camper van I reckon, pack it with tins of beans and bags of crisps, get some sleeping bags and head off. I know just the place. Port Trewithan it's called. I went there when I was about Lucy's age with my mum and dad. It was brilliant and I know the kids'll love it. It's not big like Newquay, it's quiet and the beach is small. The sea is deepest blue, nearly hurts your eyes just to look at it. But it's the sands that are magic; sometimes they're the colour of bleached bone, sometimes they're golden white, and other times they're like, oh I dunno, runny toffee. There's little bays and coves, and the kids can catch stuff in rock pools, and we can eat fish and chips every day. I've been giving it some thought. What do you say, Soos? If we're canny we can even park up for nothing. It'll only cost some petrol money and a bit of food, and we'd have to buy that anyway, wouldn't we?"

Susan shut her eyes and imagined warm Cornish sunshine instead of inner city humidity; she saw her children wearing shorts and tee-shirts running barefoot, herself in a bikini, Rob tanned and strong...

"It sounds wonderful, but I'm not sure." She heard a cat outside beginning its nocturnal serenade, and thought of listening to the sea instead. If only.

"No, Rob, we can't afford it."

"Come on, Soos, I've got a few bob. We won't need to pay for a hotel. We'll be like gypsies. A couple of weeks. What do you say? Hmmm?"

His hand found her own private cove beneath the

sheets; the tide was in, and he began to work his special magic.

Three weeks later in mid-July when Lucy's school had broken up, Susan, Rob, and the children were playing happy family in an ancient camper van. It was a relic from the 1960's, still painted in psychedelic swirls, and borrowed from Rob's friend from the pub, the boy with the wispy beard. There was no charge, Rob only had to make a delivery to some people in Launceston, and take a small package back from them at the end of the holiday. Despite Susan's reservations, which were mainly financial, the children's excitement won her over and drew her in like iron filings to a magnet. The night before they set off they could barely sleep, and Susan lay listening to them chattering away in the next bedroom. On the morning of departure Nicholas and the normally calm and mature Lucy were hopping with anticipation once all their gear was stowed.

"Are the sands really magic?" the boy asked. The questions started before they were out of London, the same questions that had been asked once the children learned of their upcoming adventure.

"You bet," Rob said.

"Are they white gold or just gold?" the girl wanted to know. She had an eye for colour, and selected her own outfits with care from her small wardrobe. This summer she favoured mint green and pale pink.

"White gold at day when the sun's overhead, then just plain gold, deep gold you might say, when the sun goes down. Yes, deep gold." He lowered his voice in the style of an American country singer. The children giggled. They liked it when he did his funny voices. Nick was sometimes 'pard'ner' and Lucy he called 'ma'am.'

"And the sea? What sort of blue?"

Rob considered the sea, the hints of azure, cobalt and turquoise that it displayed from memories of his own childhood's Cornish idyll.

"The sea," he promised, "is every shade of blue you care to imagine," and he smiled at their mother. Susan settled back into the cracked upholstery of the passenger seat and let herself be seduced by thoughts of the magic she was sure would eventually unfold.

Once they departed London, heading further west they not only left behind the stuffy confines of the small flat in a baking summer, but also the sunny rays that penetrated the urban grime. The nearer to Cornwall they travelled, the cooler it became; the clouds lowered, and the dreams of every shade of blue were replaced by the reality of several shades of grey, from pewter to dove, via battleship and ash. Once they crossed the River Tamar the first stripes of rain streaked the windscreen, and Rob discovered only one of the wipers worked. By the time they stopped in Launceston for him to exchange one large brown envelope for one small mystery parcel, the watery blobs had joined up to create a genuine Cornish downpour, and in the rear of the van the children's despondency hung like damp laundry. Lucy and Nicholas looked out of the windows, searching for the shades of blue and gold of their promised land, and the nearest they managed was the sight of a lady in a navy mackintosh running for the shelter of Boots the Chemist.

"Don't you worry," Rob said, "you wait. Tomorrow it'll be fine. You'll see. It'll be magic."

He was supremely confident, for it had never rained during the holidays of his own early years. Susan remained tight-lipped and consoled her children with milk chocolate buttons. That first night they all fell asleep with raindrops the size of golf balls bouncing off the roof of the camper van, which Rob had tucked in a corner of a municipal car park. He and Susan slept either side of the van on padded benches that also served as narrow beds, and the children were shoehorned together at the rear, behind the Formica dining table. Susan had cleaned the van when Rob brought it round the day before their departure – "No kids of mine are going to sleep in THAT," – she had announced, as she set to with Vim and bleach and a can of air freshener.

He tried to hold her hand across the gap that separated their sleeping berths, and she turned her back on him and faced the van wall. It smelled of Vim.

The next morning she awoke, stiff and cramped, in the same position. She looked at her watch: 7:15. The van was silent, its thin curtains drawn across the windows. The children were still asleep, no doubt worn out after the journey, the disappointment, and some inferior fish and chips. She turned towards Rob, but there was no sign of him, his sleeping bag was screwed in a heap on the opposite bench. She closed her eyes again and then became aware of a strange sensation, a bright light that dazzled her, even behind closed lids. Rotten sod, was he shining a torch in her face? That wasn't funny. The door to the van opened, an unaccustomed brilliance poured in and Rob shouted,

"Wake up, you lazy lot. Sun's up. Didn't I tell you it'd be magic?"

He wasn't wrong. That day and the next, and the one, two, three, four after that, and into the second week, the sun shone on them as if they were the chosen ones. Lucy and Nicholas turned from pallid West London basement dwellers to bronzed little berries. Susan lounged around in shorts and a bikini, and her blonde hair was lightened further from exposure to sun and sea. It developed the consistency of coir matting but she didn't care. Rob's tan deepened each day, his eyes a startling blue in his weathered face, and he let his beard grow. They drove to other areas and explored, they walked, they ate ice creams and the children were beyond ecstatic. For the adults only one thing was missing.

They had parked the van away from prying eyes in a quiet spot at the end of the town, where they'd not been before. The children were playing behind some boulders that lead to a series of inlets and rock pools, each one revealing new treasures. It was amazing how much happiness could be achieved with a shrimping net and a couple of plastic buckets that cost only pennies.

Rob and Susan were stretched on a towel, within earshot of Lucy and Nicholas, while still managing some privacy. He stroked her bronzing stomach, which was flat and firm.

"Unlucky for some," he said, his hand moving to her thighs, rubbing ever upwards.

"What is?"

She wasn't feeling unlucky, even though their holiday was almost over. Since her husband had been killed she had acquired the knack of savouring each precious moment, and the past two weeks had been overflowing with them.

"Thirteen," he said, parting her legs just slightly.

"Thirteen?"

"Thirteen days we've been here, and that's thirteen days without a fuck."

"Rob, shhh!" She giggled, and trapped his hand between her legs.

"They can't hear me." He leaned into her until she could smell his warm, toasted skin, and let his beard scratch the side of her neck. "We could go back to the van, nobody to disturb us. Tell the kids we're going to have a lie down because we've got a long drive tomorrow. They can see the van from here. They'll be fine."

The cunning use of his index finger in the region of her pleasure dome convinced her. Susan sat up, adjusted her bikini bottom and put on her beach cover up.

"Lucy! Nick! We're going to have a bit of a lie down, got a long drive tomorrow," she said, echoing Rob. "You know where we are, you won't have to cross a road if you want me." Lust notwithstanding, their safety was always her main concern. "All right?"

Her children were intent on their latest discovery in the pool.

"I said 'all right'?"

"All right," said Lucy, without looking up.

"We'll leave our stuff here, so help yourselves if you want an ice cream from the shop." To keep the sand out of their belongings they had hung their gear on an old rotting wooden board. She shook out their towel and draped that over it too.

"All right," repeated Lucy, then she screamed as her brother threw a tiny crab at her.

Rob led Susan towards the van. "Won't even notice we've gone," he said.

Some time later Nicholas had had enough of the rock pool. The shop that sold ice creams was shut for lunch so he wandered off to the next small inlet. It was unlike the others, a bare, flat bed of very dark sand, almost grey in colour and surrounded by tufts of coarse grass. He thought it was a good spot to build a sandcastle. He began by shovelling some sand into his plastic bucket, scooping it up and cramming it down with his hands. It was damp, not powder fine and dry, like the area where his mum and Rob had been. He knelt and concentrated, unaware of the rippling beneath him as he dug his knees in. Having packed several bucket shaped mounds together, he decided he needed some shells and suchlike to decorate them. Lucy could do that.

"Lucy! Come here, I want you."

Silence.

"Lu-cy!"

Sisters! She either hadn't heard or was ignoring him, so he'd have to go himself. He tried to stand and toppled. The sand wouldn't release him, so he made an effort to kick his way out which didn't help as his lower legs vanished into it. Next he wriggled a bit and struggled a lot and then found he was covered up to his knees. He didn't think the sands were magic any more, he thought they were naughty. Twisting his body towards the rock pool where his sister still played, he shouted her name.

"Lucy!"

The movement pulled him further down, until he was up to his waist. This time Lucy turned. She had known him all his short life and for once it didn't sound as if he was just being a pest. She scrambled over the rocks towards him, by which time only her brother's head and shoulders were sticking out of the lightly shifting mass. It looked as if the sand was eating him. He still held on to his red bucket.

"Lucy," he cried. "I'm stuck."

She was his big sister; she would get him out of trouble.

She trampled the coarse grass and jumped, launched herself onto the sand and reached for him, as he threshed and tossed and twisted and turned. A kick, a final lunge, and she managed to grab his shoulders though she was sucked down immediately by the force of her leap. He dropped his red bucket and clung onto her, burying his face in her neck. Their small thrashing limbs were no match for the relentless sand. It devoured Lucy and her brother.

"It's all right, Nicky, I'm here."

They were the last words she ever spoke.

As her eyes and her ears and her mouth filled with coarse, damp, grey grains, Lucy screamed; in the camper van her mother screamed. Neither heard the other and a red plastic bucket rolled on the surface as the sand settled. From nowhere the wind rose. It blew at the towel and the bags hanging on the rotting wooden sign, revealing some lettering:

AN ER U C SAN TA WAY

Thirty-three years later, Susan sits beside the sign on the beach. Her skin is puffy, her hair grey, and she holds an old red plastic bucket. She stays for thirteen days, unlucky for some, and the council has long since replaced the dilapidated wooden board with a new notice that is properly maintained, although the message remains the same. It is made of toughened, industrial strength plastic, perfect for all weathers, ideal to withstand seaside conditions, guaranteed not to chip or flake, warp or crack, and is graffiti proof. It is white with red and black lettering and shows a drawing of a flailing matchstick man, surrounded by a mass of speckles inside a red triangle:

DANGER! QUICKSAND. STAY AWAY.

ONCE UPON THE END

Once upon a time a young woman lived as a permanent house guest with seven bachelors. The arrangement was a loose one: the men provided for her and gave her free accommodation, while she maintained their household, and gave their hitherto chaotic lives some semblance of order.

Bianca was content to tidy up after "the boys" as she called them, even if their average age was forty-five. The monotony was one thing: clean, polish, brush, wash, sweep in the mornings, then peel, slice, shred, chop, mash in the afternoons to prepare the supper, so they could sit down to a hot meal on their return from work. The loneliness was something else. Although the boys were kindly enough and brought her small treats from the village and the latest celebrity-watching magazines to read, she sometimes wished that there was another person to talk to during the days to save her sanity throughout the relentless round of clean, polish, brush, wash, sweep. She tried having imaginary conversations with an invisible companion, but what she longed for was a real girlfriend to gossip with, about nothing in particular and everything in general. These boys however, her self-appointed guardians, they told her repeatedly to keep herself to herself, not to venture abroad unaccompanied, and not to talk to strangers.

"Lock the house after we've gone to work," said Dave, the eldest, on more than one occasion. "You never know who's out there," he would add mysteriously.

"It'd be nice to have some company once in a while," she moaned only the other night, while darning a hole in Desmond's sweater. She wasn't helped by the light source, a 25 watt bulb in an old Anglepoise lamp. The mechanism was faulty and the head tended to soar upwards, away from her work. Like so much in the bungalow it was patched and repaired and probably a fire hazard.

Gordon looked up from his *Daily Express* crossword.

"Bleedin' hell! You've got us, what more do you need?"

Bianca had to chose her words carefully. Even if they were sometimes a bunch of dull fucks – it was Gordon ironically who had taught her to swear – she literally owed them her life. Her mother died when she was a baby and eventually her father had remarried. Their house was redecorated, all bright and shiny and sparkling with mirrors everywhere, which the little Bianca had loved. But soon afterwards his new wife had turned against her for no apparent reason. Why? Had she been naughty? What had she done wrong? She remembered walking in the woods with a man, someone she knew and trusted, someone who used to work for her father perhaps? And she remembered a knife, a big knife with a long blade that caught the sunlight as he raised it over her. She remembered running, running, running, though the man had not followed. Fleeing for her young life she was, and then she remembered walking, walking, walking until she found this strange house in the trees, at the end of a rutted track. And the boys had shown her kindness, given her food, and a bed and most important of all, safety and security. It seemed ungrateful, churlish, to complain but she was a woman, so complain she did. No, what she really wanted was some girlie company, someone of her own age and sex to have a laugh with, to swap make up with, to natter and chatter with, to perhaps even venture out to the shops with; was it so much to ask?

"Yeah, but you're out all day, and I'm here on my own and…"

She got no further. Gordon snapped his biro to a standstill; this was a bad sign. It usually meant a lecture.

"We don't go out and work because we enjoy it, you know. We can't sit around doing sod all, much as we'd like to. And you don't hear us complaining." He looked around for support from his fellows, saw none was forthcoming so ploughed on. "It's a nasty dirty job, sometimes it's a dangerous job, but someone's gotta do it. And that someone happens to be us."

"Yeah, yeah, yeah. I know, it's not for the good of your elf," muttered Bianca to her sewing. But Gordon had ears like a bat.

"You having a laugh?"

He clicked his biro back into life, ready to resume battle with five across.

"If you're bored we can always find you some more chores."

Bianca opened her eyes wide in horror. "What? What chores?"

"I'll have my usual, thank you very much," said Harold, looking up from his book.

Gordon ignored him. "Must I remind you, young lady, that we're slaving away to keep you here in the lap of luxury."

He waved his hand around the large kitchen where most of them gathered in the evening, as it was the warmest room in the bungalow. His wave took in the mismatched chairs, the cracked lino, the elderly kitchen units, and the ancient Belling cooker, where only three of the four rings worked on the hob. You try cooking for eight adults on that.

Bianca wasn't sure if he was being ironic, in fact she wasn't even sure what "irony" was. Her education in some of the more subtle nuances of human behaviour had been sadly lacking. However she was saved by Bryan, who had been sitting in the corner, writing some Christmas cards. It was only September, yet he liked to start early, to be sure of missing the rush. He always blushed before he spoke; this was endearing in a boy of ten, in a man fast approaching forty it was a little odd.

"I think B-B-Bianca's got a point. Girls like a b-b-bit of

124

fun, and it's about time she b-b-began meeting a few people nearer her own age."

He reddened anew and buried his head in his address book, looking for cousin Peter's details. Piper, P, that would be. Gordon ruffled around in his chair, like a mad old rooster about to peck at something. Anything.

"What do you know about what girls like, then? Eh, what do you know? Share your vast knowledge with us. Go on then, Mr Casanova, tell us." He abandoned the crossword, snapped his newspaper into submission and turned to the sports page.

"B-b-b-b…" Bryan attempted.

"B-b-b-bugger off," said Gordon.

Dave, always reasonable and the peacemaker, said:

"Now, Bianca dear, it's only because we have your best interests at heart, that I advise caution while we're not at home. There'll be plenty of time for you to go out, start meeting young people, but not just yet a while. I know we must seem like a bunch of old fuddy-duddies, and it gets a bit boring for you sometimes…"

You don't know the half of it, she thought.

"… But please just do as I ask, stay inside and keep the place locked when we're at work." Ever the diplomat, he continued: "If you want to go off shopping or whatever it is young girls do, then one of us will go with you. Bryan, you'd like to go to Matalan with Bianca one day, wouldn't you?"

He named a big store that had recently opened, just a short walk, maybe six or eight miles away.

Bryan nodded and blushed.

"And Sid could go too, if his cold ever clears up."

He glanced over at the sorry Sid, who honked cheerfully into a giant spotty handkerchief.

That was a couple of days ago. No more had been said

since, and they had all gone about their respective routines: Gordon to his crossword puzzles, Bryan to his Christmas cards, Harold to his *Bob Monkhouse Bumper Joke Book*, and the others to whatever amused them best.

Perhaps it wasn't so bad after all, Bianca thought, on a glorious, sunny morning, as she tided up from breakfast. Golden buckets of sunlight poured in the window by the sink, caressing her arms and face as she sank her hands into the soapy water and scoured the remains of scrambled eggs from the pots and plates. They always had scrambled eggs on Thursdays. The front door was locked, as per Dave's instructions, but she had opened the kitchen window to let in some air, as the warmth of the sun was beginning to make her feel drowsy. She went back to her chore.

Scrape, scrub, wash, rinse. Scrape, scrub wash, rinse.

Sigh.

"Excuse me, dear..."

Bianca snapped to, nearly dropped Gordon's West Ham mug, and looked up. A strange woman had appeared by the open window; she blocked out the sunlight and cast Bianca into shade. Her features were obscured as the sun was behind her, but she seemed to be roughly about the same age as Dave, and a good head taller as she was almost on a level with Bianca.

"Fuckin' hell," said Bianca, "where did you spring from?"

"Sorry, love, did I startle you?"

"Yeah, a bit."

"We've just moved into the area, and I was wondering if you could give me the name of a reliable window cleaner."

She moved slightly, yet her features were still hidden. Bianca could only make out dark hair piled high and big sunglasses, like a film star. She had a nice voice, though. Soothing, educated, not from around here.

Bianca wiped her hands dry. "We don't use a window cleaner, I do the windows. It's only a bungalow, so there's no need to pay someone to do it."

"Oh well, never mind, I was just passing, and thought I'd ask."

Bianca wondered at this remark; it was hard to 'just pass' their front door, as the property was at the end of a dirt track, though it was well maintained by Dave and the others with their shovels and picks.

The stranger continued: "I saw the open window, and thought it would be nice to meet one of the neighbours. I hope you don't mind. You're quite secluded here, aren't you?"

Bianca didn't know what made her say it, some demon perhaps, but she heard herself saying: "Yeah, it's a bit like being buried alive at times."

The woman laughed.

"Come on now, it can't be that bad. It's idyllic, so peaceful, so tranquil, so..." She paused, as if searching the air for another adjective. "Yes, I daresay it is rather like being buried alive."

Bianca snorted with laughter at this, most unladylike, and the older woman joined in, sharing the moment. So then they talked about this and that: moving house, window cleaning, and the household miracle that was white vinegar; they swapped cookery tips, wondered if hemlines were up or down for winter, speculated about the likely choice of name for pop goddess Beyhanna's new baby – the smart money was on Miguel – and generally just nattered. Like girls do. It was just like having a friend at last, perhaps not one of her own age, in fact she sounded quite old, but a friend nonetheless.

Bliss!

Although the other woman seemed content enough leaning against the window ledge, angling herself against the autumn sunshine, Bianca began to feel uncomfortable about not extending hospitality to the stranger. Breeding will ultimately tell. A small voice reminded her of Dave's cautious words, however.

At exactly the same moment the woman, who might almost have been a mind-reader, said: "Shall we have a picnic? I did a bit of shopping before. I've got pitta bread and taramosalata, some cake. No, you've probably just had your breakfast. How about some fruit? There's this delicious apple, we could share it."

Bianca wasn't too sure, although she didn't want to offend the woman.

"Oh no, I couldn't really. Look, I'd love to ask you in for something but…"

"Wouldn't hear of it, I wouldn't dream of imposing on you further. And besides I'm the one that's turned up unannounced," she said. As if by magic, she produced from her bag a wonderful large apple, red on one side, yellow-green the other. A small leaf was still attached to the stalk and it quivered in the slight breeze. A knife appeared from apparently nowhere. Sunlight danced on the blade blinding Bianca for a moment, which reminded her of something that happened when she was still very young, but which she couldn't call to mind just now. She was strangely drawn by the apple and its shivering leaf. The woman sliced the fruit in half with a swift, sure stroke, and bit into the yellow-green skin.

"Mmmmm, this is so good, so sweet; here you are dear, I've kept you the nice red half, lovely and juicy, crunchy, refreshing – just what you need after your housework."

She offered the apple through the window.

Bianca shook her head.

"No, I couldn't. Shouldn't. Mustn't really."

The fruit rested on the woman's upturned palm, her elegant blood red painted nails holding it like claws. "Go on, you'll love it," she purred.

Bianca looked at the perfect half of the perfect apple. "We-ll…"

That gentle breeze again. It bore on it the scent of that

fresh apple, crisp and clean, the smell of the last days of summer. The end of warmth.

"Oh, alright then. Thank you."

As Bianca leaned forward, clouds lowered and obliterated the sun. The gentle breeze became a wind and fat rain drops fell. She took the apple and bit into the delicious fruit. She bit, she chewed, she swallowed. Its absolute impossible sweetness was a shock, like crunching a block of pure honey, cloying, but seductive. Some flies thought so too. They left the drain where they had been congregating, drawn by the apple's syrup sweet effluence and headed for the open kitchen window.

Then just as suddenly the sweetness vanished, and Bianca was left with a bitter aftertaste that washed around her mouth and flowed over her teeth and gums. Her mouth was dry, not at all moistened after the lovely fruit. Her throat felt like sandpaper, coarse and rough, constricted; her breath came in short bursts as she fought to control each one and sucked at the air. And the piece of apple she had swallowed, it stuck, blocking her gullet. She tried to cough and breathe at the same time, neither was possible and she only managed to gag and choke. She stretched out a hand through the window to her friend, Help me please, please help me. Me. Please. Help. But the woman only removed her sunglasses. And she watched. And waited.

Her face was no longer backlit and just for a moment, seemed familiar.

Bianca's last thought was: would her new friend's shoes get ruined as she walked in the rain along the muddy path?

Further down in the valley the storm clouds gathered, a flash flood hit the village and the entrance to the mine. Dave and his brothers perched on a ledge as the water levels rose. Gordon said, "Looks like we're fucked," and Bryan's last thought was: would Bianca be able to get out and post his Christmas cards?

A. REEVES TALE

The injustice of his situation was not lost on him. He, the wronged husband, the cuckold, the sorry sap, was living in a grim, one-roomed flat above a pizza delivery shop, in a less than salubrious part of town; she, the bitch, the Jezebel, the slapper, still enjoyed the comparative opulence of the marital home, in one of Nottingham's more desirable suburbs. He had left his beloved mortgage-free, three bed-roomed semi-detached house, because he could no longer bear to breathe the same air as his wife, once her betrayal became known to him. He had left because, although not a violent man, he thought he might strangle her while she slept. He had left because it was easier to pack a bag and find somewhere warm and dry to sleep, while he plotted the best course of action. And plot he did. In the workplace, his superiors had often commended him for his methodical and ordered approach, and he now fully intended to apply this precision to the thorny problem presented to him by that whore's infidelity.

His name was Alan Reeves, an uninspiring and unimaginative name for an uninspiring and unimaginative man. His wife, Janet, had said as much. She said he was boring, his job was ditto, his family likewise; she said if he bought one more taupe or fawn garment to play golf in, then she would set fire to it. And not on the brick-built barbeque, but in the Hygena kitchen that had looked very nice when fitted back in the 1980's. Before he'd packed his bag, he had made sure that his golf clubs were safely stowed in the boot of his car, a champagne coloured Vauxhall Vectra. Priorities sorted, he went back for toothbrush, pyjamas, changes of clothes, peppermint tea bags, and then left the house and the perfidious consort in leafy Sherwood Close. Until he was able to find himself alternative accommodation, he stayed with his sister, Susan. She was blind and had loathed him since an unfortunate incident with a sparkler one November 5th when they were both children. Her guide dog seemed not over fond of him either. Tucker would skulk with ears flattened and bare his teeth at him, not the expected behaviour from seeing-eye man's best friend. However the accident had taught him caution in later life, so all was not lost – apart from Susan's eyesight that is.

One wicked and weary Wednesday, Alan parked tidily in his allotted place marked "Manager," at the Job Centre near the Castle. He sat staring at the wall in front of his car. It was an ordinary concrete wall with little to distinguish it, except this morning when it became for Alan, a cinema screen. Onto this he projected an image of his wife. In his fantasy movie she was writhing in some horrible death agony that had somehow been wrought by him. He wasn't too clear on the specifics, whether she had been shot or poisoned or stabbed. Whatever the means, it seemed to cause her maximum pain though it was hard to trace the flow of blood on her Scarlett O'Harlot crimson dress. Reverie over, he locked his car, double-checked the boot was secure, and entered his place of work.

It was a charmless building, colourless, squat and drab, unrelieved by the jaunty green and yellow Job Centre sign, and therefore suitable for one such as he, a man apparently devoid of any flair or imagination. When he and Janet first met, there was a promise of a glittering career as a continuity announcer with local television. He was plucked from obscurity after a producer's wife heard him on hospital radio as the lady recovered from a hysterectomy. He had cheered her immeasurably while she lay mourning the loss of her womanhood. Although he was only a voice-over artiste, his reassuring soothing tones had been much in demand in the heady world of television. Why stop there? Janet had wondered. Network television was the next logical step on his career path. However, there had been cutbacks and on the last-in, first-out principle, new boy Alan found himself surplus to requirements and their dreams of stardom foundered on the rocks of budgetary constraints. Janet never quite recovered from the disappointment. Fortunately he soon secured himself a real job, a worthwhile job, with a pay structure and the promise of promotion and security; twelve years later and he was the Business Manager of a Job Centre, which had recently been granted "Plus" status. He reported only to the area Site Delivery Manager, and in a parallel universe he may well have been a force to be reckoned with.

This particular Wednesday all was not well at the pit-face, for a virulent influenza epidemic had laid low several of the staff. Management was expected to roll up its sleeves and attend to the Restart and New Deal clients, do the fortnightly signing, answer the telephones, and do New Claims interviews. Alan had worked his way up from a humble Fortnightly Job Search Reviewer to his current illustrious position, and pretended that it was good to get back to the "shop floor," as he sometimes called it, highlighting the phrase with quotation marks drawn in mid-air, a gesture which Janet described to her girlfriends as "naff."

Alan prepared a cup of peppermint tea from his own personal caddy, made in his own mug with hot, but not boiled water. He summoned a quick meeting with the staff members who had managed to arrive for work and delegated the various tasks, putting himself in charge of the Restart list; this involved dealing with clients who had been claiming benefit for thirteen weeks or more, and thus far showed little or no likelihood of finding employment. The building was always overheated and when the doors were unlocked at nine o'clock and they were "open for business" – cue another of Alan's air quotation marks – job seekers and claimants were joined by more than a handful of itinerants who found the indoor temperature more to their liking than the municipal benches near the Castle walls. Many weeks' worth of hardened pigeon excrement did little to enhance the appeal of this outdoor seating, for even these doughty knights of the road had some standards to uphold. Although the security guards, or Customer Care Officers as they were now called, were reasonably diligent, it was not unknown for the occasional fragrant vagrant to slip past.

Alan looked at the first appointment. It was scheduled for 9:10, a Mr Bob Loxley, and quickly read through his paperwork to check on the man's employment history. At 9:12 he looked up from his desk and called out the man's name:

"Mr Loxley? Bob Loxley, please."

A tall, lean fellow stood in front of him. He was of any age between thirty and fifty, had shoulder length hair, a small beard, and wore a long coat. It was a strange garment, slightly threadbare and in a certain light appeared to be blue, but on closer inspection, had more than a hint of green in it. At first glance Alan had taken him for one of the passing itinerants.

"Mr Loxley?"

"'Tis I."

"Right, Mr Loxley, take a seat."

Mr Loxley sat. Alan riffled through his file again.

"So, it's been a while then, hasn't it? Any luck on the work front? You've been claiming rather a long time now."

Mr Loxley shrugged, and ran an elegant finger down the front of his coat, smoothing away invisible wrinkles.

"Well, yes, I rather suppose I have."

"And I see your Restart adviser's suggested that you

might have to think of some alternative job paths?"

"Yes. I think he did." Mr Loxley seemed somewhat vague about the matter. He had the faintly irritating air of a minor aristocrat who has just pranged the old man's Bentley.

"Any thoughts then?" prompted Alan. "There really doesn't seem to be much call nowadays for a man with your," – Alan had noted the other man's preferred profession, and chose his word with care, – "your skills."

Mr Loxley sighed in agreement and offered a rueful shrug of the shoulders as if saying: Tell me about it.

A less mature staff member might have suggested that he wait for the pantomime season, when he would be much in demand, but Alan's approach to the job would brook no such frivolity.

"I have to remind you of your Job Seeker's Agreement, which you signed, Mr Loxley. You must be seen to be actively seeking work, you realise that don't you, and you must be prepared to accept alternative employment, or at least retrain for something."

"I do like to work out of doors," said Mr Loxley helpfully. "Perhaps a garden centre or something of the kind. Yes, something outside might be nice."

Nice. Not an adjective you heard every day at the Job Centre, Plus or otherwise.

"Now, that's the spirit," said Alan, "let's just have a check on the system to see if there's anything available."

He pecked away at the keyboard, but the computer seemed to be stricken by a similar virus to the one that had done for several of the staff.

"Sorry, it's a bit sluggish this morning," he said to his customer, who was examining his fingernails. The man's hands were slender and the fingers beautifully tapered. They were the hands of a person destined to hold a quill pen perhaps, or illuminate mediaeval manuscripts, or even apply vigorous brushstrokes to a giant canvas of a

Madonna and Child; they were hands that managed to be elegant yet strong at the same time. By contrast Alan's were, according to the faithless spouse, unnaturally damp at all times, and his fingers as seductive as a pound of pork chipolatas. "Skinless, at that," she had hissed. Bitten nails and shredded cuticles were further consequences of the separation.

The computer whizzed, hummed, played its indescribable tune, and the screen finally crawled into life. The operating system was virtually obsolete and the list of job vacancies was three days out of date. Alan sighed, worried at a bit of hangnail, and remembered where he was, in full public view, and not in the privacy of his small office. He ceased chewing, and wiped his hands on his light brown corduroy trousers, already worn a week, and with not much prospect of a trip to the dry cleaners. Mr Loxley stopped admiring his nails, and regarded Alan.

"Something amiss?" he asked.

Alan scanned the three-day-old list.

"No, no, not at all, just having a quick look-see, to check if there's anything suitable…"

He scrolled through the job opportunities: bar staff, waiting staff, nursery assistant (pre-school playgroup, and not horticulture), kitchen fitter, bathroom fitter, youth justice worker, dental nurse, hairdressing junior, leaflet distribution driver, recruitment consultant, waste disposal operative – now, that at least was "something outside." Alan, however, was a kindly man (when not driven to the point of insanity by a faithless consort,) and couldn't really imagine someone with the hands of an aesthete humping bins into the corporation dustcart. Parking attendant would have fulfilled the criteria, but lately there had been a massive external recruitment drive. Park-U-Rite Meter Reading Services, who supplied the council with its required number of employees, had filled their quota recently so no vacancies remained. Shame, that. No, it wasn't looking good for Alan's first client of the day. Time was pressing, because of the staff shortages. Each attendee was allowed a scant ten minutes, and the queue was growing behind Mr Loxley.

"Well, there doesn't seem to be anything right now, so I'll sign you on for the next fortnight. Next time you come in, we'll have to discuss a training course, see what options there are for you. In the meantime please scour the press, drop in here when you can, and feel free to register with any employment agencies. Remember to make a note of any job applications that you make."

Bob Loxley nodded to all of this, and signed the usual form, which was added to others on a small card, the whole held together by rubber bands. The design of this documentation had been clearly overlooked by the march of progress. He then shook Alan's hand, another rare occurrence, rose to his impressive height, and departed silently, like a blue, or maybe a green wraith.

Alan checked the man's employment record one last time, pondered a while over his "jobs sought", and wrote himself a reminder on a yellow post-it note. This he carefully folded into four and placed in his wallet, tucked behind a photo of himself shaking hands with a startled looking Ian Woosnam at St. Andrews in 2000. It replaced a photo of Janet that he had removed as soon as her perfidy was confirmed. He had stabbed and gouged it with a potato peeler before quitting the marital home.

Back to today's Restart list.

"John Dale, please, Mr Dale."

A Hell's Angel, tattooed across his face, neck, and any other part of ample flesh that was currently visible, assumed the seat across from Alan. A lurcher wearing a spotty bandanna in place of a collar accompanied him. The lurcher smiled and Mr Dale growled.

"So, Mr Dale, it's been a while then, hasn't it…"

The next two weeks were a continuation of Alan's domestic nightmare. Work occupied most of his time, but he was less than precise on occasion, and small errors were creeping in. His Site Delivery Manager and occasional golf partner, expressing some concern, let it be known that questions were being raised as to his administrative competence. For the first time in his career he was vulnerable and he wasn't sure how to react. There was little time for a relaxing game of golf, and before he fell asleep most nights he applied his mind to the problems that beset him, namely Janet Reeves and her shameless occupation of the house on Sherwood Close.

One evening he returned to Sherwood Close to collect some more clothes, as trips to the launderette and dry cleaners were not always a luxury that time permitted him. He was a hands-on sort of Manager and couldn't be popping in and out of the workplace on the merest whim. The house was deserted, but there were lights blazing in most rooms. Extravagant Janet. In their, now *her*, bedroom, the bed was unmade, and it did not take a master sleuth to work out that both sides of the bed had been in use. Frequently, judging by the smell. His wardrobe was now given over to another man's clothing. Gaudy shirts that reeked of stale sweat and some indistinguishable after-shave, pairs of jeans, and trainers and cowboy boots were thrown into the space. Alan assumed they belonged to the treacherous spouse's latest conquest from her evenings at line dancing. His own clothes were rammed into a corner; all those neatly folded jerseys in shades of mushroom, stone and biscuit, and ironed shirts, and pressed slacks. Janet had hooted with derision at the word: "What the fuck's that mean? Slacks? They're trousers, you prat," she told him between snorts of laughter. He took all he could pack into an old rucksack and some Tesco's carriers, and returned to his small flat, an infinitely depressed man, with the nascent stirrings of a plan. Gradually the germ of a solution, which had been festering somewhere in the darkest reaches of his troubled psyche, began to raise its ugly little head.

A stranger's cowboy boots were the catalyst he needed. That and a folded post-it note retrieved from his wallet.

Alan Reeves' strategy was mustered with the precision of the Normandy landings, which was appropriate as this was a kind of warfare. He plundered bank accounts and savings accounts, which he had changed to his name only once a whiff of his wife's infidelity had reached him. This caused him no feelings of guilt at all, for she had her salary from the tanning parlour to sustain her. He removed some of his paraphernalia from a side pocket in his golf bag, and therein stowed funds, mainly in used tens and twenties, for the day when...

...The day when Bob Loxley next presented himself at the Job Centre Plus. Two weeks exactly after his last visit, and Alan was lying in wait for him. In a blur of beige polyester he swooped and removed Loxley's paperwork from the staff member who was about to attend to him.

"I'll take this one," he said, leading the startled claims officer to assume that he, the Manager, was doing one of his random checks. He steered Bob, resplendent once again in his coat of blue, (or was it green?) towards a quiet cubicle, away from the babble of the main office. Bob seemed neither surprised nor intrigued. He sat when invited to do so, crossed one leg over the other, erased more imaginary wrinkles from his garment with those perfect fingers, and listened to what Alan Reeves had to say to him, regarding his job search. More precisely, he discovered how he could cease being an unemployment statistic.

When other staff members passed near the cubicle, they heard snatches of Alan's comments:

"… this could be just the opening…"

"… your skills are very specialised but…"

"… yes, you'd cease to be on the unemployment register…"

"… the public purse can't continue to support…"

These were all phrases that were in daily use at their place of work, and nobody paid very much attention. Neither was much regard given when Bob Loxley left the cubicle, left the office and left the Job Centre Plus, carrying a Tesco's bag. Alan closed down Bob's claim and typed into the overloaded, antiquated, difficult-to-search system: "Employment found. ES 40 signed. Mr Loxley will be self-employed, unspecified work out of doors, poss. gardening?"

He then took to the department shredder a stack of out of date paperwork, into which he had very, very carelessly scooped Bob's documentation, including all his signing coupons. Methodical as ever, Alan had removed the rubber bands that held them together, for their insertion would have rendered the machine inoperable. As far as hard copy was concerned, it was as if Bob Loxley had never even existed. It was as if he had been plucked from thin air like a phantasm, then vanished back from whence he came.

Two days later, the local paper published on its front page a photograph, which had been taken on a mobile phone and, although slightly blurred, was not for the faint hearted: the picture showed a body, female, lying on a pavement, and a handbag dropped beside the recumbent form. As the emergency services had not yet arrived, a thoughtful passer-by had partially covered the lady with a jacket. However it didn't lie flat over her; it was raised as if a short pole or something similar held it up, thereby creating an almost tent-like effect over her chest.

The headline read: "WOMAN VICTIM OF FREAK ARROW ATTACK." And the story that followed told the tale of tragic local beauty, Janet Reeves, aged 35, manageress of a tanning parlour, who had been fatally wounded outside her £175,000 home in Sherwood Close.

According to the paper a witness after the event claimed to have seen a man fleeing the scene:

"Mother of two, Maryanne Mallett, 24, said, "I didn't really see what happened though I saw this bloke running, well, he wasn't so much running, more sort of walking quickly. He went down the alley between the houses. Sounds daft but I said to my friend I thought he was carrying a longbow. She said I was mental. Now I'm sure. You don't expect that sort of thing to happen round here, well, do you? It's a nice area. I've got kids to worry about. He was wearing a blue coat, I think, or it could have been green."

"Police are appealing for further witnesses to call Crimestoppers on...

"Turn to page 7."

LAS COSAS QUE HACEMOS POR EL AMOR

I came from a poor family, just like her. I should have been an actress. Just like her.

With her perfect blonde chignon, there is never a hair out of place. Nor will there ever be. Of course the nose needs some attention and there I have the advantage over her. Also my feet are perfect. And I have all my fingers. You've heard the rumours that they cut one off to check it was human? Well, they're true. He was outraged by that, he said she wasn't human she was super-human, a goddess. He believed it too. He still does.

However the main advantage I have over her is that I am alive, whereas she is dead and has been these past nineteen years. I am now forty whereas she will be forever thirty-three. Thirty-three, that perfect number! The same age Christ was when he died, lest her devoted followers need any further excuse to venerate her. How do you compete with a corpse? Who was it that said "Power stands but authority sits?" I think I should amend that, for she has the power and the authority and she is lying down. What an irony. When a woman holds the power and she is on her back, it is usually for other reasons.

At first I thought he was making fun of me. We were alone, after she had been returned to him from her resting place in Milan. She had certainly travelled a lot in the intervening years since her death and had been prone to many mishaps, and invasions upon her person. He became incoherent with rage when he thought about what had befallen her, and this was bad for his blood pressure so I had to calm him, to mollify him and remind him there were still good times ahead. I dared to hope that the best times were still to come, but didn't say this to him. The flunkeys and the yes-men and the bodyguards and the tarts had all left after her arrival at our apartment, a ceremonial event and heavy with significance. Alone at last, just the three of us, he continued to gaze upon her as if she were a princess doomed to sleep for a hundred years.

"You see, my sweet Isabelita," he said to me – he liked the diminutive form – "you see, the power she wields simply by lying there, by doing nothing. Did you see the effect she had on the others? The presence, the magnetism, it's all there still."

He addressed me by name though he looked only at her. He stroked her cheek. The lighting in the room was dim but there was still a visible sheen to her skin, as if she was sweating. She wasn't of course; it was due to the wax.

After that first day when she had been safely delivered to us, he was content for me to smooth her hair, and apply some make up to her face that shone despite my best endeavours. She remained in her coffin in what had been the dining room of our apartment, high above the city that had welcomed him as a son in need. We were, we still are, protected by our wealth, our reputation and above all by *her*, that woman in the box, whose name I will not permit myself to speak. He whispered her name, as if to soothe her during a bad dream. I watched and I waited. I knew there was something coming, yet couldn't really anticipate what it might be. I'd learned some things; I learned about embalming and the works of the Renaissance masters; I learned how to tell a good champagne from a great one, and how he liked his shirts monogrammed; I learned how to stand with the body slightly angled and the weight on the back leg for a photograph; I learned how to move money from continent to continent, and how to remove those who no longer performed a useful function. I'd learned when to smile, when to be silent, when to place a supportive hand on his arm in the presence of the press. I learned acceptance.

So I waited, slim, blonde, trim, coutured, manicured. I waited for something; he was going to ask me something. But what, I couldn't begin to guess. The man was so complex, so alarming, so utterly terrifying, yet so, how should I put it, so *vulnerable*. Yes, that's the word, vulnerable. So I could never refuse him anything, I'd followed him from home to live on another continent because he needed me. And what woman can resist that? I ignored the stories about the tarts; they didn't trouble me half as much as *she* did. They may have held power over him for an afternoon or a week or a month but he was always back at my side because I was his wife and these ludicrous painted whores held no fears for me.

Unlike her.

So how do you compete with a corpse?

Answer is: you don't.

You comfort and agree and consider and listen but you put the irrational fears aside. You think your status as living makes you safe, the chosen one.

I convinced myself of this, assured myself at three in the morning when I couldn't sleep, and he slumbered and snored with two doors between us. I thought I was doing fine. Until he asked me. Rather he *told* me, for that's the way it usually was. He told me things:

"We're leaving for the country tomorrow."

"My brother's children will be staying with us for some time."

"I don't like this apartment. Tell them to find me another one."

"Your maid has a squint, it's like the evil eye. And she's fat. Get rid of her."

Yes, he told me that to enhance my own power, to make myself adored by the masses back home, I must get into the box with her, I must lie beside her and somehow absorb her charisma. And I thought at first he was making fun of me. I made light of it, though perhaps standing beside the cadaver of his other wife was not the place.

"Don't be silly, darling. I'm wearing Dior!" I said.

"Do it, Isabel. Feel her strength, understand her magnetism. Her people need you." *Her* people, always *her* people. Never his or mine.

"Juan, no, don't make me. I can't do that."

"Of course you can. She can't hurt you, she's dead. You've brushed her hair; you've tended to her already. You've touched her. Now let her touch you. Lie along side her, feel her power, feel it, Isabelita. Embrace her."

And so I took off my shoes, he helped me onto a chair, and he assisted me to stand on the dining table where the box, where the casket lay, wherein his former wife lay, the darling of a nation, cast into exile like her husband. And he helped me into the casket and bedded me down beside his wife, her tiny corpse that was wasted after cancer. She had been embalmed though there hadn't been much to work on, one of the guards told me. I lay on my side, she on her back, and settled myself as best I could. To accommodate both of us, I had to place an arm across her and rest my head on her shoulder. I tried to think that I was lying next to a large wax doll, I tried to pretend but it was no good. The wax was cold and I had to be very careful lest any portion of her snapped off.

He looked down at us, his dead wife and his living wife, and he looked peaceful, content, for the first time in a long time. He stretched out his hand, it hovered over my head and I thought he was going to stroke my hair, to thank me perhaps but it passed over and rested on her perfect coiffure. It was like a benediction. And then he helped me out of that box, and he stayed with her though I had to leave. I went to my rooms, vomited, showered, changed, and threw the discarded clothes away. Dior and Pucci I remember went into the bin with chicken bones and vegetable peelings and eggshells and I forbade any of the staff to retrieve them, as they sometimes did with unwanted clothes and suchlike. Afterwards I slept a while, then showered once more. I refused dinner.

The second time he told me to do it, I held my breath, climbed the chair and lay beside her again. I closed my eyes until it was over, and then retreated to my rooms, showered. That night we went to a charity reception at the Bellas Artes for South American orphans. I wore emeralds from Brazil.

The third time I did it after I had tended to her myself as he still requested. I sprayed my perfume, Chanel No. 5, over her corpse, and I lay down at least able to enjoy the scent. Her cotton shroud had been changed for a fresh one by the nuns who came and prayed with us, and the fabric was less unpleasant than before.

After the fourth time I retired to my rooms, summoned my new maid and had her arrange my hair into a blonde chignon. I'd already started lightening my hair, gradually so he hardly noticed, until one day:

"Oh, Isabelita, your hair, the way the sun caught it just now, like a golden halo, my darling," he said. Then he sighed. I knew he thought of the other darling.

And yesterday, the fifth time, I stood before him, elegant and groomed, with a mink coat draped across my shoulders. "Juanito, shall I lie beside her?" He was speechless with pride and joy, and merely nodded.

I made him happy.

I make him happy. Just like her.

PEACOCK BLUE DRESS

"I, Ruth Elizabeth Tyler, take you, Thomas Savage, to be my lawful wedded husband..."

Ruth rehearsed the words. She was like an actress, and although the script was short, she would be word perfect, her performance would be flawless. It was a shame he had no middle name to balance her own 'Ruth Elizabeth,' something like 'James' or 'Andrew,' something strong and traditional. No great matter but she might need to give it some thought. Anyway, Thomas's relations would melt and his harridan of a mother would accept her unconditionally. That's what true love was, unconditional. Ruth had read it in the magazines, the glossy monthlies and the down market weeklies. She would cut articles and paste them in a scrapbook. Mostly they were of special relevance to the prospective bride: wedding day etiquette; how to quell those nerves on the Big Day; make up tips to hide a ruddy complexion. This last was important for Ruth had a tendency towards the florid.

Her reverie was interrupted as the shop door opened and Major Tweed came in. It was raining and he shook his umbrella outside rather than drip on the floor of the dry cleaners. Major Tweed. A dapper fellow with a clipped moustache, eyes like raisins, and of an age somewhere between sixty and seventy, guessed Ruth. A retired military gentleman allegedly from the officer classes but Ruth had her doubts. Thomas's mother would probably describe him as 'common.' Even NQOSD, perhaps.

"Good morning, Major."

"'Morning, though I'm reluctant to prefix it with the word 'good' today."

He winked at her and Ruth smiled at the small joke.

"Particularly nasty weather, as we used to say." He

pronounced it 'par-tick-er-larly', which indicated another joke in the making, one she chose not to encourage.

"Only April showers," she allowed. To business. "Have you got your ticket please, sir?"

He produced it from a purse that was horseshoe shaped with a button stud to hold the top over the bottom section. She had never felt entirely comfortable with gentlemen who used purses for it seemed somehow unmanly. Thomas used an old black leather wallet, stuffed with photos of his intended, which thrilled her more than words would permit. She located the Major's clean cavalry twill trousers, which he checked under the plastic covering while she was busy with the till. Customers often did this, covertly checking their items when they thought she was too preoccupied to notice. When he brought them in there had been a strange stain, for which he could not account, but Ruth was used to 'strange stains' and they no longer held any interest or alarm for her. She would tell Thomas in the evenings about the procession of garments that had passed through her hands that day, and the myriad of scents, marks and scuffs that accompanied them. Stale perfume, grease, crayon, dog, biro, blood, mildew, smoke, dried vomit, paint, coffee, plasticine, pollen, curry, sweat. Odours and signs of failure, promise, deceit, desire, fulfilment, neglect, joy, rapture, despair, abandonment, fatigue. Sometimes even life and death. Each dress, skirt, coat, every pair of trousers, every bedspread, each set of curtains could provide its own small history. Ruth liked to entertain Thomas with stories of some article of apparel and create a short biography for it: where it lived, its owner, the reason it needed cleaning. For example, though she almost blushed to say it, she thought perhaps Major Tweed's mysterious mark had something to do with his fondness for watching the children playing in the park. She had seen him. She had seen how he always chose the same bench nearest the swings and sat with a mackintosh over his lap, whatever the weather. As a child Ruth had always had a fanciful imagination, which her teachers said would be her undoing. They didn't believe her when she told them how the parish priest had touched her 'down there' during a retreat. They said she was wicked, that it was a cardinal sin to tell lies about a man of God, and she would go to hell if she persisted with her tale. If they could see her now, those Sisters of Mercy, who hadn't, in Ruth's opinion, lived up to the name. They would be surprised to see her settled, with a responsible job and a good and decent man to whom she was utterly devoted, and he also to her. They would be very surprised if they could see her now.

After Major Tweed there was a slow procession of customers throughout the afternoon. The day-to-day business of a dry cleaning shop did not make for frenzied scenes. The pace was measured with small exchanges of information or comment, the handover of money, though never great sums, and the departure of a satisfied customer. The Misses Maxwell brought in the elderly faded curtains from their dining room for their annual spring clean; Mrs Riley handed in her youngest son's cricket trousers, as her washing machine and biological detergent had proved unable to shift persistent grass stains, and the season barely started; Mr Latimer came to collect his dinner suit – he was a Rotarian and was due to speak that weekend at a fund raising event. His main concern was not the quality of the speechmaking, but he was worried that the suit might have shrunk during the cleaning process. His vanity amused her, for he was a portly gentleman with thinning hair, but she was convinced that when he looked in the mirror he saw Cary Grant. Another little titbit to amuse Thomas.

To the rear of the shop, through a door with frosted glass in the upper half, there was a small kitchen, used by Ruth and also Hayleigh, the other staff member; there was a cloakroom with cold running water only, and behind that a storeroom. This in turn opened onto the delivery area for the drivers. Cleaning did not take place on the premises but, at half past four, three times a week, the delivery van arrived with a consignment of freshly cleaned clothing and household linens. These were exchanged for bundles of tagged, soiled items. There were two drivers, Terry and Lofty. Terry was tall, thin and his hair always needed washing. Also personal hygiene was not his forte. He was genial, he whistled as one might reasonably expect a delivery driver would, but Ruth was very glad when his visit was over, especially during the summer months. She had been known to spray the back area with air freshener after his departure, unkind but necessary. Hayleigh refused to take in the stock when he delivered for that very reason. She said: "Blimey, Roof, he don't half honk." Ruth despised the syntax but appreciated the sentiment.

Lofty was round and rosy, plump as a shiny aubergine in his purple polyester uniform, and a good three inches shorter than Ruth, who was five feet eight. Once or twice she had invited him to stay for a cup of tea, for he was funny and charming and sang snatches of Italian opera, which Ruth thought was very fine and indicated some degree of education. However he had spoiled it all by inviting her to a jazz club with him one weekend and she had declined, as graciously as possible. Thomas would never permit it, but as Lofty knew nothing of her paramour, she let him down as gently as a lady could, or should. For a few weeks afterwards there had been something of an atmosphere between them, much throat clearing and looking at the floor by Lofty, though gradually they learned to relax again with each other and the invitation was all but forgotten. Ruth didn't offer him any more tea though, just in case. She wouldn't be responsible for his actions.

As manager of the dry cleaners, Ruth was responsible for uncollected items; if an owner had not come to claim his or her property within three months, it was company policy that said items would be taken to the local charity shops. A notice on the front of the counter announced this fact. Customers were phoned only if there was a delay with the cleaning of their garments, a rare occurrence. This overdue stock was kept on a rail in the storeroom, and when time allowed, Ruth or Hayleigh would go to Cancer Research or Age Concern with carrier bags full of forgotten or unwanted items. Over the years Ruth, although keen not to abuse the privilege as manager, had helped herself to a few garments and Hayleigh had a keen eye for any additions to her somewhat eclectic wardrobe. However she had recently taken an evening dress, a straight sheath in peacock blue silk. It was simplicity itself. She remembered well when its owner had brought it in: Ms Weinberg, an American woman who was based in London for six months working with a finance company. She had worn it to a retirement dinner for their London vice-president, and some 'asshole' – to quote the lady – had seen fit to pour half a bottle of Merlot down the front of the dress, which had apparently then lain ignored on the lady's bedroom floor for a week before she could 'find a window' to take it for cleaning. It had not been delivered back when expected as the Cypriot family who actually did the stain removal, decided it needed a second clean before it could be passed as satisfactory. Ms Weinberg was not best pleased to discover her garment wasn't ready and fretted that she had to 'find another window to pick up' before she too was scheduled to return 'Stateside,' as she called it. That was months ago. An ocean, a continent and several time zones now separated that disagreeable woman and her beautiful dress. Ruth had since removed the long pin that she had carefully hidden by the armhole, placed in such a way as to give the unsuspecting wearer a very nasty scratch. It was a small revenge for any customer who had displeased her, and a tactic rarely employed despite the satisfaction it gave her when she imagined the moment when... oh, yes, very pleasing indeed. She kept the dress tucked away at the back, its peacock blue sheen hidden by other duller items. It was in her size and would suit her perfectly. Thomas would be enchanted. She had found for him a dinner suit, unclaimed as its owner had died in a road accident a few days after his wife had brought it in for cleaning. Ruth felt it tactless and insensitive to advise the new widow that her beloved's finery was ready, and after three months it too was placed on the rail in the back room, soon after the widow had moved back to Cirencester to be near her parents. It fitted Thomas as if made for him. Thus two peoples' misfortunes were other people's good luck. Such was the way of the world.

At half past five Ruth locked the shop door, relieved that the day's work was done and she could at last relax and look forward to her evening. For it was to be a very special one. She first tidied away any remaining tickets, safety pins and stray buttons from the counter. Ruth marvelled at the carelessness of people, pockets often revealed a prize or two and once she had even found a diamond earring in the inside pocket of a gentleman's jacket. She noted the customer's name, and locked the gem away in the shop safe. When he came to collect his jacket, she produced the earring and she said she had discovered it while giving the pockets a thorough examination. She did this automatically, patting down each garment like an airport security guard. He virtually snatched it from her before a lady, who addressed him with the intimacy of a wife, joined him in the shop. Ruth and the customer exchanged the merest glance, and as the couple departed her shop, the gentleman stopped at the door, ushered his wife outside, and nodded to Ruth. Whether this was in gratitude or conspiracy she could not be sure. Thomas thought him a thorough rogue when he heard the story and Ruth naturally agreed. Also she liked the way he said 'thorough rogue,' like a hero in a Victorian novel. She imagined he would want to 'horsewhip the fellow' too. He had such a way with words.

Having tidied the shop, she then retired to her private domain. She closed the half-glass door on her sanctuary and began her preparations: the lighting was not perfect, but she had brought from her home a small table lamp which now sat on top of the fridge. This was kinder, more intimate than the overhead strip light. She had also a CD player and selected music by Nat King Cole, a particular favourite of Thomas's. From the fridge she produced a bottle of Tesco's dry sherry and poured two glasses. Her excitement was growing – Thomas was due soon. They were going to a dinner dance, he in the dress suit for which Mr Stanley no longer had a need, while she would be resplendent in Ms Weinberg's peacock blue silk. How handsome they would look, how envious the others would be, especially the ghastly Jennifer Marsh, who was sure to be there. She had been engaged to Thomas previously though he told her she had only been a passing phase – like teenage acne, he said, attempting to turn the sorry event into a joke. He was very considerate like that.

Ruth tidied the table where she had had her solitary lunch, and replaced papers in a folder marked MY BIG DAY!! Some of these she would later transfer to her scrapbook, marked OUR BIG DAY!!! She hoped the three exclamation marks weren't too vulgar, but it was the only way she knew to express her excitement as the happy day drew ever closer. There were recipes for intimate suppers; ideas for honeymoons (although she knew that was Thomas's province really;) articles from bridal catalogues, old papers and magazines. Among the pile there lay a yellowing cutting from a newspaper, a wedding photograph. The man was smiling and handsome but the woman was indistinguishable, for her face had been cut out and a crudely drawn dagger dripping crayoned gore protruded from her chest.

The scene was set. Now it was time for Ruth to get

ready.

She took the evening dress from its plastic cover, went into the staff rest room, washed her face and hands and removed her work clothes, which she folded. She sprayed herself with Estée Lauder Youth Dew, a favourite scent for years. She slipped the dress over her head, and smoothed the fabric over her very slender frame. She swapped her flat-heeled daywear for a pair of patent court shoes. Round her neck she fastened a triple strand of pearls, her parents twenty-first birthday present to her, and now well past their own twenty-first birthday. She brushed her hair, dusted some powder across her cheeks, and made up her lips twice, remembering to blot between applications for lasting effect. She had read that in one of her magazines. Standing back from the pocked mirror, although she was not a vain person, she admitted to herself that she did look very fine indeed!

She checked her wristwatch – nearly 6 o'clock. She placed a bowl of cashew nuts to the left of the glasses, then moved it to the right. Then back to the left. Thomas would be here soon, they would have their sherry, they would talk over their wedding plans for while, and she would show him the photographs of a possible venue for their reception. Then they would leave for the dance, where her very presence would make Jennifer Marsh curdle with envy.

6 o'clock. Ruth unlocked the door of a storage cupboard and withdrew a male shop window mannequin fully dressed for a black tie event. It was a strange old dummy with painted hair, a chipped nose, and dirty alabaster complexion. Fixed blue-grey orbs stared at nothing. She manoeuvred it to the back door, propping it awkwardly, so it was slightly bent at the middle and with one hand resting on the doorknob. She went back to her CD player, raised the volume as Nat King Cole announced that though laughing friends deride, tears he could not hide, and she turned round suddenly.

"Thomas, darling," she said I didn't hear you come in..."

ALMA MATER

Now it is a luxury development of lifestyle apartments with an on-site gym and a concierge; in the nineteen-sixties the convent of Stella Maris in Romsey was a boarding school for girls aged eleven to eighteen. A large picture of the Virgin Mary spreading her blue cloak like celestial wings dominated the entrance hall and gave the school its motto: *Sub Tuum Praesidium*. Under thy protection. Converted from a vast Victorian house with a jumble of later additions, it was unwelcoming and unforgiving then whereas now it is double glazed and desirable. Halogen lights create intimate corners in the individual apartments; Apple computers glow seductively; granite worktops sleekly gleam, and antiqued leather sofas placed on floors of reclaimed burnished oak create a pleasing ambiance for the residents. Commute over, the building is a haven from the workplace, a veritable sanctuary where the demons of the day are exorcised. Now.

Then. The building was home to an order of teaching nuns, the bequest of a devout spinster who died in the middle of the nineteenth century. Despite the warm red brick, mullioned windows and gabled roofs, by the early nineteen-sixties the convent school was a cold, forbidding place. Spartan and sunless, with badly lit hallways and corridors and an antiquated heating system, it offered little in the way of comfort to the pupils who were separated from their families during term time.

On school days during break periods, the junior girls congregated out of doors. As they were not quite children, yet still not women, the Sisters hoped they would burn off some of that terrifying prepubescent energy. The older students were allowed to remain inside ostensibly to study for their 'A' levels, though more usually they would droop around and moan about the boyfriends they had left behind. Or compare and contrast the relative merits of their favourite Beatle.

Because of their age, twelve year-olds Louise, Barbara, Jennifer and Karen were meant to spend their recreation periods outdoors. Only torrential rain would permit them entry to the relative warmth of the gymnasium. On days that were cold but dry, they wore coats and scarves outside and ran around more than usual to keep from freezing. Louise, their leader, thought this was barbaric and would hug a temperamental radiator before being shoo-ed outside with her peers. Then one day she happened accidentally upon a warm spot indoors that she thought might provide the perfect refuge.

It happened thus: she had been to swimming lessons in the town with her class. Upon return the usual procedure was to take wet swimwear to a special small area called rather grandly the Drying Room. The space measured some 4 feet by 12 feet and was at the end of a long, dark corridor; it was windowless and very warm because of the antiquated heating pipes that ran its length. Racks of pegs had been attached to the walls for damp towels and black regulation bathing suits. There was a light switch on the wall outside which Louise flicked on, while she looked for an available peg. As the door closed behind her, the 20-watt light bulb flickered and went out. She was not one to panic, and felt her way in. The door opened again and there was her friend Karen fiddling with the switch. Ever the joker, Louise draped her towel over her head and extended a hand to Karen to drag her into the darkened space, while she gave a shuddering, low moan, in the manner of a ghoul from a horror film. No one heard Karen's scream, Louise's snigger, or her terrified friend's shriek that turned into laughter. Silly Tom, the school janitor-cum-handyman-cum-dogsbody pushed a broom in the vicinity yet paid them no heed. How could he when his head was still full of that place called the Somme? Although nearly fifty years past, its noises and its colours were all he knew: rocket flares and artillery advance, white; dead horses in the trenches, blue; the place where Victor Cotton's head had been, red. And so on.

"Listen, Karen," said Louise. "The weather's horrible. We could come in here during breaks and keep out of the cold; we'll stay lovely and warm and they'll never find us. I don't know why I didn't think of it before!"

The pair reported back to their other friends, Barbara and Jennifer, and also to fat little Geraldine who was hanging around, as she so often did. She wasn't really in their gang for although pretty enough, she was too chubby and asthmatic for their tastes. Sometimes she was allowed to tag along when one of them, usually Barbara, showed her a little kindness. And she shared her sweets and her transistor radio, and often helped with their Latin or French homework.

So the girls gathered in the warm and musty hole while their peers shivered outside. To avoid discovery, they had to confine their visits to days when none of the other classes went swimming, yet enjoyed it all the more for that self-imposed restriction. Besides it gave them something to look forward to. It became an event. Karen came with crisps, Jennifer brought pop and they let Geraldine bring toffees. They always put the light out lest one of the prefects catch them hiding, and Barbara provided a torch for emergencies, so once their eyes grew accustomed to the dark, it was fun. Geraldine, although desperate to be included, was a little nervous about the venture. Hadn't they heard the story about Sister Bernadette, she asked, the old blind nun whose ghost walked the corridors? Maybe even this very one. The tale of the sightless Sister was part of school legend, though some of the seniors put it down to propaganda. The girls were banned from visiting parts of the building that were not included in their daily routines and individuality of expression was not encouraged. The Drying Room was merely for the storage of swimming kit, it was not a recognised recreation area. Louise gave the nuns some headaches as she was often caught in places she was not meant to be. The detention she had earned for talking to the gardener's boy was the talk of her year for some time.

"Nah," she said, "it's just the old girls trying to put the frighteners on us, stop us having any fun."

She was not entirely wrong as fun was a commodity sorely lacking at their seat of learning.

"You think?" asked Karen. "It could well be true. Didn't they say the Sister had a wonderful singing voice and sometimes you could hear her singing the Ave Maria?"

Unseen by Geraldine in the confined space she nudged Jennifer, who was happy to continue in similar vein.

"Don't know about that, but I heard when it was a private house years and years ago there was some story about a bride who was buried alive in the walls in her wedding dress." Jennifer warmed to her theme. "She was bricked up by a mad husband. He thought she'd been unfaithful to him before the wedding."

Geraldine did not disappoint them with her gullibility.

"No!" she gasped. As she reached for her inhaler, the other girls roared until Barbara assured her it was only a story. Still they were all rather glad to be out in the daylight and the fresh air afterwards. Bricked-up brides and blind nuns indeed!

A few days later, the girls were once more taking shelter from the fine November drizzle that turned the hair of their classmates to nut-brown fuzz. Once they were settled on their nests of dried towels, Jennifer, the literary star of her year, said, "I came across this tale about a blind beggar and how he took his revenge on a boy who had stolen from his begging bowl. It happened in London, years ago when it was still really foggy. He recognised the robber from his smell and knew he could follow his scent. Anyway, one night the robber was walking home with some more money he'd taken from the poor box at St Vincent de Paul's."

Geraldine said that it was terrible to steal from the blind and the poor too.

Louise shushed her and bade Jennifer continue.

She told them how the robber heard the tap tap tap of the blind man's cane in the fog, and every time he stopped and turned to check who was following he could see nothing. Tap tap tap, then stop, turn, still nothing. Tap tap tap. All around him the fog swirled and thickened, and the street lights gave only spectral outlines of distant buildings; a dog howled somewhere – even Louise shuddered at this – yet still, tap tap tap.

"Who's there?" said the robber.

Tap tap tap.

"Show yourself!"

Tap tap tap.

"Why are you following me?"

Although he quickened his pace the tapping still continued. He started to run; he ran down a side street, then another, losing his bearings and slipping over the cobblestones that were damp and greasy. Stopping to listen, all he could hear was the river slapping against the boats, and the sound of a ship's ghostly horn somewhere on the water. And always:

Tap tap tap.

Because he could see only inches in front of him he didn't realise how near the river was, or how low the embankment wall was, and the tap tap tapping grew closer. He stumbled, fell into the water, and because his pockets were so full of stolen coins he sank quickly, dragged down to the muddy bottom by the weight in his pockets. There was no one else to hear his attempted cries and once the robber's desperate thrashing was over, the blind man turned and walked away.

Tap tap tap, finished Jennifer.

They all were quiet.

"Wow," said Louise at last.

"Jen, that was horrible," said Karen, full of admiration. Typical of many twelve-year-olds, they welcomed the frisson of fear in the dark because soon they knew it would be light again. Barbara's torch shone on all the girls' faces as they breathed once more, though Geraldine sat open mouthed and fumbling for her inhaler.

"Relax, Geraldine, it's only a story," said Barbara. And they all, even Geraldine, laughed at last.

For their next visit as they huddled together surrounded by drying towels and swimsuits, Karen took her turn with the storytelling. She thrilled her small audience with a Gothic tale of a strange priest who came to say the Mass, and fed communicants real blood and dried flesh from children he'd murdered. As she described the moment when one young innocent was slain with a hunting knife and pieces of his body were cut up into bite-sized portions, Geraldine actually screamed out loud. Sister Benedict happened to be thereabouts, looking for Silly Tom to perform some other mundane task. The nun flung open the door to the Drying Room to find five girls sequestered there during the lunchtime break.

They were summoned to appear before Reverend Mother who issued lines, penances, principally in the form of decades of the Rosary, and banned them from entering the space again, other than to hang their damp swimming togs. She saved her flintiest gaze for Geraldine, at whom she was particularly surprised and not a little disappointed. A prolonged spell in such a place was injurious to her fragile health and she was seriously minded to inform the girl's parents.

"You will confine yourselves to the prescribed places at the appropriate times. We cannot, we shall not, permit you girls to wander around the school at will. It is for your own good. You would do well to recall the school's motto," said the Superior.

A week or two passed. In December the temperature dropped, sleet fell, and the junior girls were permitted to spend their recess hours in the vast assembly space of the gymnasium. They still wore their coats indoors, but finally there was shelter from the fiercer elements of the weather during the short days leading up to Christmas. Louise felt it would be safe to resume visiting their favourite haunt; they would not be missed in a gymnasium heaving with young girls killing time in the dinner break.

She said that the stories would continue, and they were to take on a new tone as a result of the dressing down from Reverend Mother. Henceforward all must feature nuns as the victims or villains.

Louise herself decided to kick off the new regime. To add theatricality to the proceedings, she took a towel from the rack, and placed it over Barbara's torch, which she held under her chin. A ghastly green light suffused her face and she was unrecognisable, with sunken eye sockets and hollowed cheekbones. The scene was set for the story of Sister Marinella from the Philippines and her evil voodoo doll. With its shadows thrown on the convent walls, greatly magnified by some trickery, it frightened the Mother Superior into a heart attack, which Louise described in all its awful detail. A similar fate befell her successor and ultimately Sister Marinella became head of the convent. However one night as she was in the chapel alone, she too was visited by this horrible sight, this giant silhouette. The thing was beyond her control, and she was found the next day, features twisted into a howl of fear and her eyes staring madly at some distant spot. At her side was a small broken puppet doll.

Brilliant, they all declared.

Louise asked Geraldine to prepare a tale for the next session, but she refused, she didn't think she had the imaginative flair. Also her time was otherwise engaged as she had chosen to transcribe the stories from memory and planned to give each of the others a copy as a surprise Christmas present. It was a lot of work, five copies in all including her own, though she felt it would be worth the effort and the others would be pleased. If she couldn't add to the collection, at least she could give them all a keepsake.

So it was the turn of Barbara. Her story concerned a deranged nun who was the only survivor of a war. All the Sisters in the tales by definition were deranged, damaged or just plain evil. She stayed on in the ruins of her convent, eking out what little food she could find and praying for deliverance. Weeks passed by and one night the Devil appeared to her in a dream and told her if she wished to continue with the Lord's work there was only one hope of survival for her: she must drink the blood of innocents. Very soon after, some children who were fleeing the advancing armies took refuge at the convent. She shared her bread with them and made them comfortable as best she could, and when they were asleep she slit their throats. She caught the blood that flowed in a chalice salvaged from the ruined chapel and drank her fill. And as more small groups of children came in search of sanctuary, her health and strength continued to improve. Until one day she drank the blood of a poor little boy who had a terrible sickness and his blood was infected. She too fell victim to the infection and died alone, covered in horrible sores and crying out for God's mercy.

Shudders of approval all round.

When they were gathered for their next session, they waited for Karen who had still not joined them. They only had the lunch break hour and an afternoon of rehearsing Christmas antiphons and parsing French verbs loomed. They sat in the dark on the beds made from dried towels wondering where she was, for time was precious.

There was a sound of running feet, the door opened and in she burst.

"Look out girls, they're calling the class registers and going to do a fire drill in the gym in ten minutes, so get a move on, we'll have to pretend we've been in there all along!"

After some furious scrabbling around, the girls scooped up pop bottles and crisp packets, which they rushed to stow in their lockers. There was no time to tidy up the towels, and they made it into the gym just as Sister John Bosco rang the bells to announce the fire drill and called everyone to their assembly points. Though Geraldine was a little red-faced after the slight panic, part of her enjoyed the thrill of nearly being caught out a second time with her friends. She was one of them! She belonged at last!

As she prepared for bed that night, she checked her inhalers. There were always two, an extra one in case the first should fail, the consequences of which were too awful to contemplate. There was one on top of her bedside table, and the second, which was always in or near her school bag, she couldn't locate. She went through her pockets, turned her satchel upside down, and rearranged all her exercise books and bits of paper, including the loose leaves of the story collection. Nowhere could it be seen.

While the other girls brushed their teeth and said their night-time prayers, Geraldine mentally retraced her steps that day. The inhaler. Where was it? Was in it the dining hall? The gymnasium? Had she dropped it when they ran to the muster for the fire drill? No, if she'd dropped it or left it some place, someone would have found it and handed it in. The pupils and staff were aware of the importance of her small life support system.

Where could it be?

Could it perhaps... oh no, not there! Not in the Drying Room! She couldn't go there, not now, it was late!

However there was no choice.

She hissed over to Barbara. Too much chatter in the dormitories was forbidden.

"Bar, could I get a lend of the torch for a bit?"

Barbara handed it over.

"What's it for? If you want to read in the bed you won't get far, I think it needs a new battery, it's getting faint."

"I only want to look over the verbs for tomorrow; I don't think I've got them off right..."

Geraldine was the star French pupil, so this didn't quite have the ring of truth to it, but aged twelve Barbara was not yet the astute judge of character she was to become in later years.

"Okay. Don't let it die on you though."

"Cross my heart, Bar," said Geraldine. And she did.

She waited until most of the dormitory was settled, and looked over her verbs to pass the time. Then just after eleven o'clock when all was silent and dark, she slid from the hard cotton sheets and scratchy woollen blankets that made up her bed, put on slippers and a dressing gown, and set off for the Drying Room.

A building in the dead of night, however familiar during daylight, can be a foreign country to the most stout-hearted, let alone a small asthmatic girl armed only with a flickering torch. Corridors become unnaturally long; corners conceal unknown perils and must be approached with caution. Sounds are magnified, mouths are dry and pulses race. She pushed all thoughts of Louise's story and the voodoo doll's giant shadow from her mind.

Geraldine sent up a silent word of thanks to St Christopher when she reached her destination on the ground floor. There were no windows at this end of the corridor, and had there been, it would have made precious little difference as the night was moonless, and as black as the raven's wing. The silence was palpable, not even Silly Tom's broom could be heard, nor the slightest rustle of a nun's robes, nor yet the whispered clack of rosary beads that hung from their belts. The night was cold, but she wiped moist palms on her dressing gown and fought the urge to gasp in short fast shallow breaths.

As Geraldine opened the door to the Drying Room, the torch winked, once, twice, then died. She switched on the light, hurried inside lest someone, a nun or a prefect, be patrolling and switched it off immediately, though she left the door open a tiny crack to relieve the unremitting darkness that would otherwise envelope her. She gave the torch a shake and mercifully it shone once more. Directing it across the floor area among towels and swimwear, the inhaler was not immediately apparent. She switched off the torch to save what little of the battery remained, then dropped to her knees and felt around.

From somewhere beyond, from the inky stillness of the convent, there came a sound. Geraldine listened. It was of a voice, though not quite a human voice; it seemed too wavery and high-pitched. At first she wasn't sure even if it was human, so distorted was it by the walls and corridors and the distance it had to travel. She stopped scrabbling on the floor a moment to concentrate on it as it became stronger. Clearer.

And closer.

Then the footsteps. Faltering, irregular steps. As if someone was unsure of their passage perhaps. Or couldn't see where they were. Cheated of the light, not unlike little Geraldine herself.

Finally she could hear the voice properly: it was the

purest soprano, perfect in pitch, singing a hymn.

Ave Maria.

Geraldine made out the words:

"*Sancta Maria, Mater Dei*

Ora pro nobis peccatoribus...

Nunc et in hora mortis nostrae. Amen."

It was the most beautiful thing she had ever heard.

The singing stopped. The footsteps stopped. Just by the slightly opened door to the Drying Room.

No other sound then except breathing; unlike the purity of the singing voice, this was deep, rasping, and jagged. Whoever it was, it was as if they had forgotten how to breathe. Her own breathing now in shallow pants, her mouth as dry as bone, Geraldine stood and switched on the torch for whatever illumination it might provide.

The door opened wider, ever wider, and she shone the pencil thin beam on the long dark folds of a sleeve. But the fabric was ragged and had marks on it, crusted indefinable stains. As the door was opened fully she trained the light from the arm to the body, and clad in rotting raiments from the charnel house, there stood what once had been a nun, shrouded by a foul and fetid odour, the stench of decomposition. The tunic, the wimple, the veil, all were tattered, smeared and mildewed with filth from decades in the tomb. The face was not a face, nor was it a skull; it was in some unholy place between the two. Blackened, leathered flesh still adhered to it, and small brown teeth showed in the open maw that was the mouth; the torch's dying light revealed shrunken lids half closed over milky eyes, like dead opals. The thing, the nun, blocked the doorway, its head turned slowly this way, slowly that, as if searching for something. The creature stretched a hand in, scraping at the air between herself and the child, reaching towards her. Not so much fingers, withered claws, that may have been fingers once, pecked at the space as the nun leaned in and brushed the cheek of the small girl.

When they found Geraldine several hours later, it was not possible to do anything for her. Her crumpled body was wedged inside the door to the Drying Room, one hand holding a torch and the other outstretched, mere inches from her inhaler. Police and medical examiners were summoned, questions were asked in the most reverential of tones, and all protocols duly observed. The nuns washed her, dressed her, and laid her out in the sick bay to await her parents. They placed rosary beads in her hands, but her father removed them and flung them across the room as he beheld his only daughter. All her belongings were hastily packed up by Sister Ursula, her form mistress: some exercise books, her missal, her clothes, her transistor radio that was permanently tuned to Radio Luxembourg. She had smuggled it into the school, her one small act of defiance. Also, there were several handwritten copies of what appeared to be horror stories. As they were not official schoolwork, Sister Ursula presumed they were rubbish and placed them in a wastebasket.

At Geraldine's requiem Mass, Sister John Bosco sang the Ave Maria, her voice piercing the chapel's dusty air.

It was a sweet soprano, though not as sweet as another.

WAITING

Mrs Wilson said typical. You make an appointment and when you get there they say the doctor's out on an emergency, an elderly patient. And not a word of an apology. She was right of course. Still it can't be helped. She'd given me a lift and was going to come back after she'd been shopping. I don't like to put people out so I said, no, the bus is fine.

"It's just as well my friend's not really sick," she said. "Where would she be then?"

I had a little smile to myself. The doctors told me angina could be very serious if not 'monitored,' - that was the word they used. Yes, monitored.

"And after she went to the trouble of phoning. Right, Edna, I'll see you later."

The door shook when she left.

"She doesn't mean anything," I said to the receptionist, "it's just her way."

I heard myself start. My husband said I went on too much. People weren't interested, that I didn't always have to explain everything, so I'd tell him, "Well, Len, I like to clear things up. I don't want to feel there's ever been any misunderstandings."

"Bloody hell, woman," he'd say, "you should go and work for the United Nations, go and sort out them Arabs and Israelis, clear up their misunderstandings. Ha!"

"Take a seat in the waiting room, Mrs Gould. I'll tell you when the doctor's back," said the girl.

I don't like fusses or atmospheres. They can set me off; they make me nervous. I can feel my heart beating faster and my face gets red. It's this blessed angina. Doctor Cavanaugh saw me twice a year but this new doctor says I need an examination every three months. Very insistent, he

169

was. He looked at my notes from Doctor Cavanaugh and said, "I see you've been referred from Leeds. I was a student there."

I said, "Yes, we lived in Leeds, in Chapeltown. My husband Len worked for the Gas Board and we moved there thirty years past, nineteen sixty-three, or was it sixty-four? Going from Lancashire to Yorkshire, he said that Geoffrey Boycott had better watch out. You see he loved his cricket, and he enjoyed a joke, did Len. Anyway, he died nearly three years ago, it'll be three years come November. I'm coming back to my roots I suppose you'd call it. Manchester born and bred, that's me."

Go on, Len would have said, tell him your life history why don't you? Mine too while you're at it.

The doctor didn't seem to mind. He stroked his beard and he listened. Not many people do that any more. And he looked at me, really looked at me, like I was a person and not just a patient.

Funny, this waiting room reminds me of the front room at our home in Leeds. I daresay it's because the surgery's in a house. It's got a tiled fireplace and hearth. A picture rail. That's nice. I like a picture rail, it saves the walls. And the windows, with the metal frames I never cared much for; ours were always running in the winter months when it was cold outside. Every morning I'd have to wipe away all the water that had collected in the bottom of the panes, or they'd rust up and Len would have the painting of them in the spring. I wanted double-glazing, but Len wasn't so keen. He said it were a waste of money. He wanted to keep his nice little nest egg for when he retired, though he didn't get to spend that much of it. Always very cautious with his money, my Len. Anyway I've got double glazing now in my new flat, that and central heating. "Welcome to the twentieth century," our Carole said.

I thought I'd see more of her and Jamie when I moved back to these parts. Especially with Jamie being my only grandchild. Still, she's got that big house to look after, and Jamie. And Edward of course. I said to Len, "Fancy, our little Carole married to a bank manager!" Then there's the twins from Edward's first marriage, she sometimes has them to stay. I've not seen them since he and Carole were wed, twelve years ago. The twins were very little then, about four, running around, getting under everyone's feet at the reception. Len wanted to take his hand to them, but I told him that they were just excited, what with being bridesmaids, and getting to wear those lovely powder pink dresses and patent shoes. I think they were wearing nail polish, and they had pierced ears too. At four! I had my work cut out keeping them away from Len.

I said to him afterwards, "They were double trouble and no mistake! They kept me on my toes, I'll give them that."

"You need your head looking at, running round after them like a blue-arsed fly."

We were in our hotel after the wedding. I'd been a bit breathless, and started having twinges in my arm, then this tight band round my chest. The next thing you know, I was in an ambulance going to the Royal Infirmary. All wired up I was, and there were such a fuss. I don't like to make a fuss, I don't like to put people out, but all the doctors and nurses were ever so good. It's my own fault; I've always carried too much weight. I should have done something about it when I were young so I've only myself to blame.

Len were livid. He'd spent good money on the room, and we had to stay the night in a hospital. They let me go next morning, although I had to go for tests when I got home. I said the hotel might give him a refund as we'd not slept over, and he said I shouldn't be so stupid, they didn't operate like that. We'd unpacked, and used the soap and towels when we freshened up after we arrived, so there was no way we were going to get any money back.

I didn't want Carole told because it would have spoiled her special day. She and Edward left early the next morning for the honeymoon in Mauritius. She sent a postcard, signed 'Mrs Edward Lloyd!' with a big exclamation mark which I thought was ever so funny. Len wasn't that amused. He were never that keen on the name 'Edward,' thought it sounded way too plummy.

When we first met Carole's intended, Len said,

"Welcome to the family then, Ted, or should we call you Ed?"

"Neither if it's all the same. I prefer Edward."

"Well, that's telling us," said Len.

I went to put the kettle on.

I wouldn't mind a cup of tea right now. My mouth gets dry when I have to wait and see the doctor. I can't always remember everything I'm supposed to tell him, and something is always bound to come back to me when I'm at home. Mrs Wilson said I should write things down, and I said I'd feel silly reading from a list about all the times I had a little twinge, or got a bit out of breath. Besides, you don't want to trouble the doctor with every last thing, not when there are seriously sick people out there. I was lucky to get an appointment, and I wouldn't want to think I was taking up his time unfairly. No, that wouldn't be right.

A cup of tea would be nice though, maybe with a slice of Battenberg, then I could relax and read one of these magazines. I wonder who brings them in. I wonder if the doctor's wife reads them, or the other patients? I used to get *People's Friend*, and *Woman's Weekly*. Len liked the *Daily Express*. We had the papers delivered, until he decided he'd walk down to the newsagent for them. Why pay a delivery charge when you've got the use of your limbs, he said. And it saved on a Christmas box for the paperboy.

Not that he was able to get out much the last year. He was hardly eating, fighting for every breath, and the oxygen cylinder was never far from reach. It wasn't much of an end for him. They were very kind at the respite care place, and offered to have him stay so I could get a little break, but it didn't somehow seem right to leave him in there, and I don't think he was all that keen. He said it were noisy and there were always someone coming or going, always people standing over him, checking if he wanted anything, when all he really needed was to be left in peace. So I kept him at home.

Carole visited, and our Steve came up from London but it was just as well they didn't stay long. They would have got on his nerves. I'd have liked the company, mind; it's hard being on your own watching someone die, someone you've been with for forty-five years.

It might have been nice if Carole had brought Jamie to see his granddad one last time. She said she didn't want the boy upset, and she wanted to remember her dad like he had been. I thought, and do you suppose I don't? Don't you think I don't want to remember him on our wedding day, so big and strong and handsome as he was then? At the end he were only seventy-two but he looked ten years older, his skin was too big for him, it were grey, and his eyes looked cloudy all the time. I know it's not a nice thing to say, but his eyes reminded me of a fish's on a slab, when it's not very fresh.

Steve drove up from London with his friend. The friend went off to do some shopping while Steve stayed an hour or so. He'd grown his hair and pulled into a ponytail. Len said, "What on earth do you look like? You look like a bloody girl, that's what."

"Good to see you too, Dad," said Steve. He had on this scarf, it was made of some silky material, and he kept tying it and untying it, fussing with it like an old woman. His real name was Stephen, with a 'ph.' When he started on his hairdressing course, he told us he wanted to be called Stefan. Len didn't like that.

"We gave you a perfectly good name. What do you want to go and change it for? Stephen, now that's a man's name. Stefan? Sounds like a bloody poof."

We didn't hear from Steve much after that, though sometimes he sent pictures of his hairstyles cut from magazines. He won an award once for doing somebody's hair in a contest at the Albert Hall, I think. He's been very successful. One of my neighbours saw a photo of him in the *Daily Mirror,* he were with one of the girls from *East Enders,* or perhaps it was someone from *Coronation Street,* and the caption referred to him as 'celebrity crimper' whatever that's supposed to mean. It's a different world.

I could almost be in our old front room again. This is about the same size. We had a three piece suite instead of these hard seats. Len's chair was opposite the television, right by the fire. We only used one bar, but when he were sick we'd leave another bar on as he was feeling the cold more then. Mine was near the window, and the sofa was against the wall behind the door where they've got a fish tank here. Len had his chair and I had mine, and the sofa was for visitors. Funny isn't it, how people end up with his and her chairs; I mean a chair is just a chair really, though after a while one of them takes you on, sort of shapes itself to you without you realising it. Like shoes. Yes, it's funny that.

Len died in his chair. He'd been really poorly for a while, and we had the nurses in. They even stayed overnight so I could get my head down for a few hours. I needed to keep my strength up they said.

Mrs Harris next door, she lost her husband some years before. Her son came over to see her every week. He'd take her out, or do any odd jobs.

She had him help me make the front room into a bedroom for Len when the stairs became too much for him. He got himself up and dressed most days, with some help from me or one of the nurses. He was a proud man my Len, he didn't like people to think he couldn't do anything for himself any more. The doctor arranged for a commode, so

174

he'd have a bit of a wash in the kitchen and do his business without me or the nurses watching his every move. A man needs his dignity.

We'd had the six o'clock news on and I was waiting for the weather forecast to be over before I went out to make us some tea. We always watched the weather forecast, I don't know why as it never really made that much difference to us, we weren't keen gardeners or anything like that. We only had a small back yard and it didn't get much sun which were a shame. I think I might like to give gardening a go now; there's a little patio just outside the lounge in my new flat, and it gets lots of sun. Len hadn't made his usual comments on the news or the newsreader. "What has she done to her hair? She looks like the wreck of the Hesperus." That was one of his favourites. He was clawing at the arms on his chair, as if he was trying to hang on.

I knew then.

"Len, love. You let go if you want to. If you're ready. It's alright," I said.

He nodded. He was agreeing with me, the first time in forty-five years, and then he sighed like he was very, very tired.

And that was it.

I stayed with him and I held his cold, old hand. If you'd given me a hundred pounds I couldn't tell you when that last happened. We weren't given to displays. We'd taken our vows, and didn't feel the need to let everyone know how it was between us.

We waited until the nurse came. It was Hazel that night. She sat me in the kitchen with a pot of tea and some biscuits from last Christmas; they were in a blue tin with a snow scene on the lid. Then she went into the hall to make some phone calls, closing the door between us.

I can remember everything: the picture on the biscuit

tin, the knock on the door when Doctor Cavanaugh arrived, and then the police – Hazel told me they had to come – then another knock when the men came to take Len. She closed the kitchen door, she wouldn't let me see, but I heard one of them, it was quite a young voice, say,

"He weighs nothing this one, just a bag of bones."

Someone told him to shush.

She thought somebody should come and stay with me and wanted to phone our Carole. I didn't want anyone, I said, and besides Mrs Harris was only next door if I felt a need. So she washed and dried the cups and put everything away, then she went too.

It was about ten o'clock. I put out the lights and went to bed.

Downstairs next morning I went into the front room. I looked at Len's chair, and there was a dent where his head had been. I put my hand on it expecting it to be warm and of course it wasn't. It smelled of his hair. That smell and the hollow in the headrest; that's all that was left of him.

You're a silly old girl, Edna Gould, bringing all that up again. You should know better at your age. It's this room, isn't it, because it's like your old house, that's all it is. And because you're sitting in here on your own. If there were other patients it wouldn't be so bad, not that you'd talk to them. No, that wouldn't be right. When people are waiting to go and see the doctor, they don't want some stupid old woman chattering to them about this and that. They're not interested, they've got their own problems, that's why they're here. Len would tell me I should go and see someone about my head, not my body, carrying on like that, living in the past. He'd say it weren't healthy and he'd be right. Next visit, I'll come and wait with the others. I mean, what's so special about me?

And besides, the doctor's a busy man, I don't want to

waste his time. It's good of him to see me outside surgery hours, and all because I'd had a little turn last week.

Mrs Wilson insisted.

"Get on that phone. If you don't, I will. You've paid your stamps all your life. It's your due."

That's the kind of thing Len would have said. I wonder if they would have got on? Len would probably have thought she had rather a lot to say for herself, he never really cared for that. I don't know what Mrs Wilson would have made of him; I haven't told her much, and she's hardly talked about her husband, but she's been widowed a lot longer than me. We're not like the young folk today though; we aren't always talking about feelings and emotions. Some things are private and should stay that way.

She means well. She was very kind when I moved in. It was a raw day, late January and she had tea and biscuits for me and the removal men.

She kept her front door open just in case I needed anything. Carole was going to lend a hand, but she and Edward had to go away, a week-end break in London. A hotel and a show.

They say that you want to return to your roots as you get older. Nearly two years after Len passed, I went to an estate agent and told them that I'd decided to move back to Manchester, to Hyde. They spoke to their Manchester office and they told me they had a lovely ground floor flat for sale. Mrs Harris knew about my plans. She said she'd get her son to take me over to see it and I think she liked the idea of me doing something without telling Carole. She had a heart of gold Mrs Harris but wasn't backward about speaking her mind and she told me once she thought Carole could do a lot more for me than she did. I hope I never gave the wrong impression about Carole, it's just that she's always got a lot on.

Anyway, Mrs Harris got her Andy to drive me over. The

flat was perfect, and everything the old house wasn't; it had big windows, and central heating, a built in oven in the kitchen and a patio off the lounge.

The For Sale sign went up outside mine and Len's in Chapeltown and I bought number eight, Cedar Gardens, Hyde. I was well provided for, what with the sale of the house, and Len's pension. Funny, last visit the doctor asked me if I had any money worries. He said it was often a concern for some of his older patients and he seemed relieved when I told him I was comfortable. It was nice of him to ask, wasn't it?

I bought new furniture, new curtains, new pots and pans, new everything. I even bought a continental quilt. Mrs Harris had one and said it put paid to bed making. We still talk. I told her I were thinking about taking a holiday abroad, a short break somewhere with Mrs Wilson. I must look out my passport. The last time I used it, Len and I went to Holland for the tulips. That was nineteen eighty seven, our fortieth anniversary. I loved all the purples and yellows and reds and pinks, all mixed up. Len said we could have stood outside the local florist and saved him the money.

I'll get some bulbs for the patio, something to look forward to next spring. Moving back here is the best thing I could have done. I've got a nice modern flat, good neighbours, and Carole and Jamie not that far off. I'm feeling much better. I am really.

Was that the door? Yes, it was. It must be Doctor Shipman back from his emergency.

Good.

Soon it'll be over, then I can go home and get that cup of tea.

ABOUT KATE FARRELL

Kate Farrell lives in Edinburgh. She was an actress for over thirty years, in a career that spanned everything from Chekhov to *Chucklevision*.

As she is pathologically indisposed to describe a happy ending, she now principally writes 'contes cruels' wherein bad things happen to bad people; sometimes the innocent suffer too. Several of her stories have been published: in Charles Black's *Black Books of Horror*, Paul Finch's *Terror Tales, The Screaming Book of Horror* and *Best British Horror 2014*, both edited by Johnny Mains. Kate's debut novella *My Name is Mary Sutherland* was published by PS in 2014. *And Nobody Lived Happily Ever After* for Parallel Universe Publications is her first collection of short stories.

Two of her stories, *Mea Culpa* and *My Name Is Mary Sutherland*, have won awards, also one sonnet and one haiku. The opening chapter of the novel *Or The Cat Gets It* won the Linen Press award for their Beginnings Competition.

For further information check out the website: mynameiskatefarrell.com and for updates try her Facebook page: *mynameiskatefarrell*.

Parallel Universe Publications

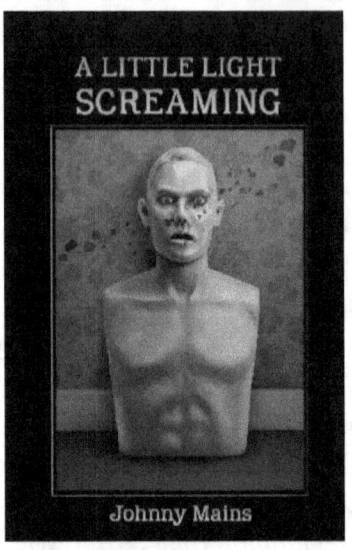

A LITTLE LIGHT SCREAMING by Johnny Mains
ISBN: 978-0993288852

ENGLAND 'B': 90 MINUTES OF HELL by Richard Staines
ISBN: 978-0993288876

AND NOBODY LIVED HAPPILY EVER AFTER by Kate Farrell
ISBN: 978-0993288883

FISHHEAD; THE DARKER TALES OF IRVIN S. COBB
ISBN: 978-0993288869

KITCHEN SINK GOTHIC: Selected by David and Linden Riley
ISBN: 978-0993288838

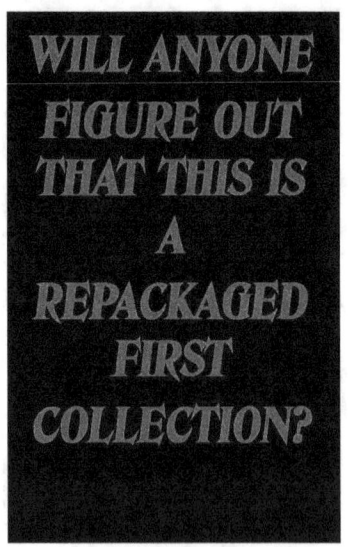

WILL ANYONE FIGURE OUT THAT THIS IS A REPACKAGED FIRST COLLECTION? by Johnny Mains
ISBN: 978-0957453579

BLACK CEREMONIES
by Charles Black
ISBN-10: 0957453558

HIS OWN MAD DEMONS:
DARK TALES FROM DAVID A. RILEY
ISBN: 978-0-9574535-8-6

THEIR CRAMPED DARK WORLD
by David A. Riley
ISBN: 978-0-9574535-9-3

THE HEAVEN MAKER AND OTHER GRUESOME TALES
by Craig Herbertson
ISBN: 978-0-9932888-2-1

GOBLIN MIRE
by David A. Riley
ISBN-10: 095745354X

THINGS THAT GO BUMP IN THE NIGHT
edited by Douglas Draa and David A. Riley
ISBN-10: 0957453566

CLASSIC WEIRD
selected David A. Riley
ISBN: 978-0-9574535-3-1

MOLOCH'S CHILDREN
by David A. Riley
ISBN: 978-0993288814

Check our website:
http://paralleluniversepublications.blogspot.co.uk/